Threads

JIA KALITA

ISBN 979-8-89544-896-0

Contents

Foreword

As I delved into the stories of Threads, I was immediately transported into a world where the familiar transforms into something uncanny and the personal blossoms into the universal. Jia Kalita has woven a remarkable collection that captures the essence of human existence—our longings, heartbreaks, and indomitable spirit. Each story, while anchored in its own unique space, resonates with shared experiences, whether through realism, fable, sci-fi, or poignant moments of deeply-felt introspection.

What struck me most about Kalita's storytelling is her skilful crafting of subtle twists and unexpected endings. These surprises unfold organically, as if each story was destined to reach its conclusion, without taking recourse to postmodernist gimmickry. While echoes of Jhumpa Lahiri's exploration of diaspora and identity tropes are subtly evident in some stories, Threads establishes its own distinctive voice, one that is finely attuned to the rhythms of urban life and the often-inscrutable pressures of a consumer-driven world.

Kalita's choice of words is another highlight of this collection. Her controlled, precise, and minimalistic style allows the weight of emotions to emerge naturally. There is a profound beauty in her restraint—every word carries significance, reminding us that true art often lies in simplicity and the space it creates for readers to discover their own meanings.

Set mostly against urban landscapes, these stories explore the alienation and distractions of modern life, yet they remain deeply intimate. The city acts both as a backdrop and a catalyst, amplifying the inner conflicts and quiet yearnings of its inhabitants. Jia Kalita's Threads is not just a collection of stories; it is a reflection on the fragility and resilience of the human spirit. It encourages meditation on the invisible threads that connect us to the world.

Reading this collection left me with a profound sense of connection, as if I had ventured not only into the minds of Kalita's characters but also into my own heart. Threads stands as a testament to her talent—affective, poignant, inventive, and deeply resonant. It is a remarkable debut that invites exploration into the intricate realm of human experience, encouraging us to reflect on the shared vulnerabilities and strengths that bind us all.

This collection is not merely a literary tour de force; it is an intimate journey into what it means to be human (or interestingly, non-human) in a complex world, leaving an enduring impact that invites contemplation long after the final page.

Prof. Mridul Bordoloi
Head Department of English
Dibrugarh University
Assam, India

Sheltered

A Rainy Day that changed two lives forever

She came into my life on a rainy Saturday afternoon. Our eyes met through the tinted glass windows of the nearby coffee shop. She was a regular there, and although I had noticed her before, I never mustered the courage to walk up to her. I would quietly observe her from a distance, noting her various moods — some days, she was brimming with joy, and other days, as gloomy as the monsoons. Dark brown curls crowned her face, adding to her dreamy, longing look. Something about her made me pause every time — maybe it was the way she absentmindedly stirred her coffee or the loneliness in her large, brown eyes.

I don't suppose she noticed me until this afternoon as I walked down the old street, seeking shelter from the downpour. Even though I saw her first, I could tell she felt the same recognition when her eyes met mine. Amy wiped off her tears hurriedly, looking flushed after realizing I had seen her a moment too soon, and quickly put her phone into her purse. She was clearly embarrassed of having let her guard down in public. The city was supposed to be her fresh start, a place where she could reinvent herself. But sometimes, one long-distance phone call with family was all it took for the tears to come unbidden.

Today was one of those days. As Amy looked into the eyes of the stranger watching her, she felt a strange mix of vulnerability and confusion, like a soul connection had appeared unexpectedly and at the right moment. After drawing one last sip from her coffee, she stepped out, umbrella in one hand and purse in the other, tiptoeing towards me in her boots, narrowing her eyes. Her mouth curved up in a soft smile when she was less than two feet apart. My heartbeat subsided as I relaxed, acknowledging her smile. At that moment, I knew my life was about to change forever. *Finally*.

As we got to know each other, I learned about her past and why she moved to this city. Amy had left behind her familiar life of the past twelve years in her homeland for better career opportunities. Initially, she was captivated by her new surroundings, exploring charming cafes, finding new spots to visit every weekend, and marvelling at the stunning skyline.

During the first six months, she immersed herself in every sight, sound, and smell of this new life. After a smooth, successful apartment search, she poured her heart into setting up her new home, infusing every corner with personal touches. Thrift store finds repurposed as bookshelves and end tables added unique character, transforming the bare, empty box into her sanctuary.

Weekdays were a whirlwind of activity as she navigated her way to the new office, occasionally grabbing a bagel or two. Her attempt at building a social circle included going for happy hours with a few colleagues and pilates or pickleball during weekends. Amidst the city's intoxicating energy, life gradually started falling into a rhythm. The same things that had thrilled her a few months back appeared mundane now, and a sense of loneliness began to creep in. Making friends and meaningful connections in a big city took work, especially for someone in their late thirties.

She found solace in a nearby cafe, a few blocks from her building, aching for familiarity. The waitress always greeted her warmly, inquiring about her day and knowing her order by heart. She was sipping her go-to caramel latte, lost in thought when our paths finally crossed today.

We walked along the wet pavement, grateful that the rain was receding. It turns out Amy hated getting drenched in the rain, too. *Compatibility,* I mused. She was more introverted than I imagined, and I did not intrude.

Over the coming days and weeks, I uncovered the little details of Amy's life — like, how blasting loud music actually calmed her nerves down or how she worked hard at a job she didn't like. She told me about her past dates and how she hadn't found the 'spark' with anyone.
"It's puzzling how this city is overflowing with people, yet I feel isolated," she said one morning while flipping an egg over a pan.

She'd often come home exhausted, flop onto the couch, and stare at the ceiling, muttering, "Just three more days until the weekend", as if those words were a mantra she clung to for hope. Then her eyes would soften as she looked at me and said, "At least I have you". I never said anything; I just patted her for reassurance. Most nights, in the silence of her cosy apartment, she whispered to me, *"What if I never truly belong here? What if this was a terrible decision I'll regret even more later?"*

Household chores were our private bonding time. While I listened intently, she'd talk about her day, ranting about this colleague or project. Sometimes, she'd pause mid-task to look at me, a thoughtful expression on her face as if pondering how I always seemed to know when she needed company. Going on walks wasn't my favourite activity, but I enjoyed that we stopped at the grocery store on the way back, where Amy would methodically pick out vegetables, fruits, and a few treats. I'd follow her through the aisles, and she would occasionally glance my way, a soft smile playing on her lips. It was clear she found some comfort in my presence.

Over the next month, Amy began to relax more, finding joy in the minor, routine aspects of her life. The familiarity of her daily coffee, the friendly chit-chat with the cafe staff, and my presence—these small comforts made her days brighter, she said. Slowly, Amy's loneliness faded. She swapped long walks for long drives and made a few friends while volunteering at a local animal shelter, where her love for animals deepened. She always did love strays. She began hosting game nights at her apartment to rekindle an old hobby, with laughter and conversations echoing through her home long into the night.

One such night, as we sat together on the couch after the last of her guests had left, tired and slightly drunk, Amy looked at me with tenderness in her eyes. "You know," she said softly, "I don't feel so alone anymore". She reached out, her fingers finding that perfect spot behind my ears.
"Maybe it's a good thing that I moved here".

I leaned into her touch, a deep rumble of contentment rising from my chest. As Amy drifted off to sleep, her hand resting gently on my back, I wanted to tell her that, frankly, I was the one who was glad she had — after all, it was my territory she had wandered into, and I had decided to adopt her. Instead, I purred in contentment, my soft, dense fur nestled against my human. With one final stretch and a long yawn, I curled up at her feet, my tail wrapping around me, ready to sleep.

And who knows? Maybe one day, she will bring home someone who would finally have that elusive 'spark'. Until then, I'd be right here, whiskers and all, happy we found each other that rainy afternoon.

DreamStream

Who are we when we lose control of our dreams?

The morning light filtered through the sheer curtains, casting soft shadows across Emma's bedroom. She blinked, her eyes heavy with the remnants of yesterday's mascara. Stretching lazily in bed, she allowed herself a moment of quiet before the world intruded. Her phone buzzed with a familiar reminder, *'Time to get on DreamStream, lovely'*. With one last languid stretch, she pushed away the covers and stepped out onto the balcony. The breathtaking view from there never failed to soothe her soul. Yet, something was bothering her, like an undercurrent of restlessness beneath her contentment.

As she stepped into the kitchen, the sleek espresso machine on the counter beeped to life, sensing her presence. Her fingers brushed the machine, and it hissed before dispensing a dark brew. With practised ease, Emma poured the coffee into a delicate, handcrafted porcelain cup, pausing momentarily to inhale its delicious aroma. These were the finest Arabica beans she had ever tasted. Her friend, Kitty, had gifted them to her after her recent trip from the Middle East.

Emma settled into her plush *Ralph Pucci* custom armchair at the centre of the living room, letting the soft fabric envelop her body. Placing her cup aside, she reached over to turn on the large, holographic television, scrolling to the latest broadcasts on *DreamStream*™. She was eager to watch Jenny's latest dream, hoping to catch a few glimpses from her latest trip. The screen flickered to life, displaying

Jenny strolling leisurely through the streets of Rome, vivid and tantalising in its detail. Emma raised her eyebrow after spotting something was off on the screen. Her expression quickly turned into a vicious grin once she found the mismatched, unpolished detail on the choreographed scene that her friend had clearly forgotten to edit before uploading. Only a true expert of the tool could have identified this subtle flaw; Emma held a glint of pride in her eyes. As she sipped her coffee, Emma absentmindedly scrolled through the rest of the broadcasts on DreamStream™.

DreamStream™ was a revolutionary technology that started as a research project designed to capture and analyse dreams, offering users insights into their subconscious minds. What had once started as a personal dream diary had become a public stage—a place where dreams were shared, curated, edited, and monetised. Naturally, the most stunning visuals attracted the most eyes.

Emma had mastered it, turning her nights into a spectacle of opulence. Her followers expected nothing less than perfection, and she was all too eager to oblige. She collected followers like bees to honey with her meticulously curated visions showcasing an extravagant lifestyle—from opulent galas and exclusive yacht parties to whimsical flights over her sprawling penthouse. Each dream experience was designed to reinforce her public image and status among her peers.

But today, something felt off. The usual excitement she felt before uploading every morning was absent, replaced by a gnawing unease she couldn't quite place. Just then, a notification from DreamStream™ popped up on her sleek screen. *Would you like to edit your dream before uploading it?*

She paused, contemplating whether to review and edit the dream before sharing. Emma played a snippet of the dream, where she had embarked on a glamorous space voyage—a theme so routinely grandiose in her profile that it bordered on mundane. With a dismissive yawn, she tapped 'auto-upload,' skipping any potential edits. Feeling certain it was another flawless entry in her digital dream diary, she got up and continued her day.

However, as she proceeded with her day, her device began to buzz incessantly with a barrage of notifications. "Is your account hacked?" read one message. She froze, staring at the stream of reactions and comments on her latest DreamStream™ upload. Something had gone horribly wrong. Messages, ranging from concerned to outright offensive, flooded in, with some accusing her of being a fake socialite. She was too shocked to respond to any calls or messages, and before she realised what had happened, there was a sharp drop in her number of followers. Her high-society circle, secretly taking vicarious pleasure in her downfall, reached out feigning concern. "Emma, are you alright?" they asked.

She frantically logged into her account to figure out what on earth was happening. Emma's face turned pale as she replayed the dream. She shook her head in disbelief when she saw herself—not in her usual elegant attire, but in a tattered hoodie, racing through a dystopian cityscape. Her luxurious space voyage had morphed into a nightmarish escape from monstrous digital glitches, her refined features replaced by the scrappy appearance of a young twenty-something man surrounded by digital demons. It was some Dylan's dream, who went by the username, 'CreativeChaoticDreamer'. *How could this have happened?* Emma cried in disbelief.

After several frustrating calls with customer support, she learned that a system upgrade the previous night had caused this catastrophic mix-up, merging her dream with Dylan's disorderly subconscious. To add to her agony, they informed her that the situation could not be easily reversed, as the dream had already gone live. Furious, she threatened to sue them if they didn't find a fix immediately.
But when she hung up, she realised, to her horror, that the damage was irreversible. Millions of viewers had already seen the video.

Panic set in as more notifications poured in, friends and followers alike questioning the authenticity of her image. Once the darling of her social circle, Emma now found herself on the outskirts, shunned and isolated. The irony was palpable; Emma, the self-proclaimed expert on spotting deception, was now under intense scrutiny and became a subject of mockery. Overwhelmed by humiliation, she buried her face in her hands and sobbed until tears marred her beautifully painted face.

Determined to reclaim her reputation, Emma decided to track down Dylan, the unwitting co-star in her dream debacle. She immediately put her online sleuthing skills to use and found his address. A few hours later, Emma stood in front of a rundown apartment building on a starkly different side of the city. It was a far cry from her world of luxury—a stark reminder of how far she had fallen in just a few hours. Anxiety and resolve filled her at once as she reminded herself that she needed answers and a way to fix this mess.

The dimly lit hallway smelled faintly of pizza and old socks as she approached Dylan's door. Emma hesitated outside the door, her fingers trembling slightly as she reached for the buzzer. A few moments later, the door creaked open. He looked every bit like his username suggested: a tousled mess of hair, baggy clothes, and an air of chaotic creativity.

"Uh, can I help you?" Dylan asked, his voice lined with confusion.

"Are you CreativeChaoticDreamer?" Emma asked, trying to mask her disdain.

It took him a few moments to recognise the reference. "Yeah, and you are…?" he answered, raising an eyebrow.

"Emma. Emma Sinclair," she said, pushing her way inside. "We need to talk."

His eyes widened in recognition.

Emma sneezed as soon as she stepped into his apartment. It was a cacophony of clutter: empty soda cans littered the floor, discarded game controllers were scattered everywhere, and relaxed cats dozed on mountains of comic books. The walls were crowded with sci-fi posters and video game art. A strong, unfamiliar smell filled the air, making it hard for Emma to keep her composure.

"So, what's this about?" Dylan asked, closing the door behind her.

"My latest dream on DreamStream- "Emma couldn't help but wrinkle her nose, "-it got mixed up with yours. My followers are freaking out."

He burst out laughing. "Oh yeah, I saw that one. Gotta say the transition was hilarious."

Emma's eyes flashed with anger. Seeing this, he quickly cleared his throat and straightened his hoodie. "So, what do you want to talk about? Wait.. you think it was my fault?"

"No!" Emma retorted. "It was a system glitch. But we need to fix this. Fast."

"Umm.. okay, how exactly?"

"That's why I'm here."

The duo would host a live DreamStream™ event in collaboration, blending their worlds through a new dream narrative that would combine Emma's lavish lifestyle with Dylan's gritty creativity. Although she felt confident it would work, Emma was gnawing her teeth minutes before the live stream started. She could not risk another blow to her reputation after the previous mishap had turned her into a laughing stock. None of her friends spoke to her anymore. The stakes were higher than ever. The idea of being seen as anything less than perfect was unbearable. She tried to shrug her thoughts off, glancing at her reflection in the ornate mirror and adjusting her hair and makeup one last time before announcing to herself, "Alright, Emma, it's time to reclaim your status. Let's do this!"

As the countdown to the live stream ticked down, Emma's heart raced. She had spent years building her image, ensuring that each post, each dream, and each public appearance was flawless, but now she was stepping into uncharted territory. *What if Dylan's messy energy overshadowed her polished persona? What if this gamble cost her everything?* She glanced at Dylan, who seemed completely unfazed by the pressure. His casual confidence only made her more anxious. But there was no turning back now. With a deep breath, she forced a smile as the cameras went live.

The live stream started, and as expected, millions tuned in. Forcing a confident smile, Emma joined Dylan, ready to face her audience with a mixture of hope and apprehension. She cleared her throat and began, "Hello, everyone. Thank you so much for joining us today. I know many of you were surprised—uh, let's be honest, shocked—by the dream I shared yesterday. I want to address that directly."

She glanced at Dylan, who gave her an encouraging nod. "As some of you may know, there was a system glitch during the DreamStream™ upgrade, which caused a mix-up between my dream and Dylan's. It led to a rather... unexpected narrative. But this mix-up gave me an idea. Instead of seeing it as a setback, I saw an opportunity to collaborate and create something unique."

Emma paused, gauging the audience's reaction through the incoming comments. "Dylan here is an incredibly talented visual designer", she continued, trying to sound as authentic and sincere as possible. "His creativity and vision are remarkable, even if they are a bit different from what you're used to seeing from me. So we decided to blend our worlds for this special event. We hope you enjoy this new narrative as much as we enjoyed creating it."

With that, Emma stepped back, watching the viewer count climb and feeling a spark of hope that this unexpected collaboration might just win back her audience's favour.

The new dream began with Emma's pristine villas, where guests in exquisite gowns and tuxedos mingled beneath crystal chandeliers. Suddenly, the scene shifted, morphing into Dylan's chaotic digital landscape. The same elegantly dressed guests navigated a futuristic cityscape, teaming up against cyber bugs and rogue AIs in a heroic attempt to save the world. The contrast was stark yet mesmerising, as the seamless transitions highlighted the beauty and chaos inherent in both worlds.
Emma and Dylan took turns narrating their parts of the dream, adding personal anecdotes and playful banter. The result was a captivating storyline that resonated with viewers, showcasing the unexpected synergy between two seemingly opposite lives.

Before they knew it, it became a sensation and love poured in:

"Oh, what a brave girl!"

"Impeccable direction!"

"Kudos to Emma for being authentic!"

"Fantastic visuals. Stunning."

Relief washed over her like a cool breeze on a hot day. She had done it. Despite all her fears, the event was a success, and the audience adored their blended narrative. The praise was not just for the dream itself but also for her courage to embrace something different, something real.

Emma leaned back in her chair, letting the tension drain from her body. She hadn't realised how tightly wound she had become until that moment. The adrenaline that had kept her going all these years, driving her to maintain an impeccable image, was finally ebbing away. For the first time in what felt like forever, she allowed herself to just be—no pretences, no masks, just Emma.

Dylan turned to her, a satisfied grin on his face. "See? Told you it would work," he said, offering her a fist bump.

Emma laughed, a genuine, unguarded laugh that surprised even herself. She returned the gesture, feeling a strange camaraderie for, perhaps, the first time in her life. "Don't forget I was the mastermind behind this", she teased, grinning back at him.

As the event concluded, it did more than salvage Emma's reputation; it catapulted her to new celebrity status. She received an influx of positive messages from viewers and friends alike. Dylan, too, found a new platform for his work, receiving several requests for virtual dreamscape design. Once again, she was the beloved socialite.

A month later, Emma awoke to the soft hum of the morning. The sunlight warmed her face as she stretched out in bed, deeply content over another restful night's sleep. She felt the comfort of her new routine settle over her like a warm blanket. There was no rush to check her notifications, no urgency to craft the perfect online persona. Somehow, she had learned to appreciate the unfiltered experiences that made life richer in ways DreamStream™ could never capture.

Wiping the remnants of mascara from her eyes, she reached for her phone and began scrolling through the notifications. First, there was a text from her friend Sara: "Babe, we all noticed how Oliver was flirting with you at the party. Call me? x" She giggled and scrolled on. The following notification was from DreamStream™: *Your dream is ready to be uploaded,* but she barely glanced at it. It was the subsequent notification that caught her attention. As she sat up in bed, she opened it with a mix of surprise and curiosity.

It was a message from Dylan: *"Hey Emma, I've got a new project and would love to collaborate with you again. What do you think?"* A smile spread across her face as she quickly typed out a positive response. With a contented sigh, she set her phone aside and decided to linger in bed a little longer.

For once, everything else could wait, and that was perfectly okay. Slow, uninterrupted mornings were the absolute luxury, Emma chuckled, pulling the soft sheets up around her as she drifted back to sleep.

The Wine Stain

When grief becomes a debt that cannot be cleared

Maya closed her laptop and buried her face in the pillow, stretching out as she exhaled the tension from her shoulders after another long workday. Two hours of uninterrupted work had left her eyes burning from the computer's glare. She tried to dismiss the memory of her boss, Anna, and the unfairness of being saddled with last-minute tasks on a Friday afternoon. *Such unnecessary stress!*

She sighed wistfully, thinking about the comfort of her previous job, where even her colleagues were more to her liking. Back then, her boss had been Louisa, a cheerful and understanding leader who always had a kind word for everyone. Louisa made the office feel like a second home, often organizing impromptu coffee breaks and light-hearted team meetings that made the workday fly by. Working under Louisa felt like being part of a family, and Maya often found herself missing those days.

How much longer could she endure this new job? she wondered as she sat up in bed—But that was a problem for Monday. Right now, all she craved was a relaxing bubble bath with her husband, just as planned. A smile lit up her face as she imagined Ralph's pout, his typical expression of displeasure whenever she was late.

Oh, the wine! She suddenly remembered—he had asked her to bring it.

Her footsteps echoed through the spacious three-bedroom apartment as she entered the kitchen, their favourite spot in the house. They had meticulously designed it to evoke an antique charm—dark mahogany shelves adorned with delicate filigree, a collection of mismatched vintage crockery, and even an ancient grandfather clock Maya had found in a thrift store and hung above the refrigerator. The simple wooden table with four dainty chairs held countless memories of shared meals after work. Over the past two years, they had transformed this space into a cosy haven, building their life together one piece of furniture at a time. Their marriage had been a seamless transition from their year-long courtship because they were perfectly compatible, sharing the same outlook on most things—except, perhaps, Maya's penchant for colourful clothing.

As Maya reached for the wine bottle, a fond smile tugged at her lips, bringing back memories of the countless evenings they had spent together in this kitchen. Cooking meals together was a cherished ritual on late nights after work. Ralph always insisted on being the sous-chef, happily chopping vegetables with the precision of a surgeon at work. It never failed to amuse her. They'd often play their favourite jazz album and dance around the kitchen, waiting for the sauce to simmer. Those moments were pure joy, filled with the kind of contentment Maya had always dreamed of.

With a gentle sigh, Maya pulled out the wine bottle, carefully tucked away among her mother's inherited plates on one of the shelves. That bottle was a treasured souvenir from their trip to France six months earlier, and they had reserved it for a special occasion. As she cradled the bottle in her hands, she reflected on how much had changed since then. Maya had eventually come to terms with the incessant calls and notifications that punctuated Ralph's life as a doctor. What had once been a source of annoyance had evolved into something she accepted as an inevitable part of his demanding profession.

One windy July evening, while sharing a bowl of mac and cheese and watching their favourite show on TV, Maya broached the subject of their long-overdue vacation.

"Summers are approaching. We should plan that trip we've been talking about," she suggested.

Ralph grinned. "You mean our honeymoon?"

"Exactly! We both need a break."

"Agreed. France next month?"

Maya smiled. "I'll look at flights right away."

The following day, Ralph submitted a five-day leave request. After months of gruelling work, he welcomed the prospect of a vacation. Their itinerary would celebrate multiple milestones: their first wedding anniversary, the completion of his training, and their postponed honeymoon.

* * *

France

It was a sweltering afternoon when they arrived in Bordeaux, France, eager to explore the world of wine. Maya was relieved the rain had subsided; the previous day's downpour had nearly derailed their vineyard plans.

She wore a beautiful yellow summer dress that had not seen the light of day since her college graduation. City life had relegated her summer wardrobe to the back of the closet, but she had made sure to pack it all for this trip. "Miss Sunshine," Ralph had affectionately called her as he stood on their hotel balcony that day, watching her braid her damp hair under the sun.

Their cab awaited curbside, ready to transport them to the train station. The day's itinerary was packed: a village walking tour, visits to multiple châteaux, cheese sampling, and at least one or two wine-tasting classes. While Ralph wasn't the quintessential tourist, he was game. The blazing sun, however, made him question his enthusiasm. Perhaps a poolside book Perhaps, reading by the

pool would have been more appealing. But he shrugged it off, deciding to embrace a relaxed pace. They reached twenty minutes before their train departure. "Coffee?" Ralph asked, spotting a nearby café. Maya nodded, still exiting the cab as he paid off the driver.
"Bonne journée!" the driver chimed cheerfully.
Maya stood outside the coffee shop and watched as Ralph placed their order. Even from a distance, she could tell he was trying to speak French to the cashier. His mouth always appeared exaggerated when he used a foreign language. The café was filled with lively chatter, creating a fitting ambience for the bustling terminal. They walked around, holding coffee in hand and their arms linked together.

"I'm happy we're not rushing around like tourists," Ralph remarked, sarcastically, as he enjoyed a croissant. "Slow travel is better."

As if catching the hint, Maya squeezed his arm. "No more hectic trips, I promise."

Seeing a look of relief wash over his face, Maya punched him playfully.

They reached the vineyard just in time for their tour. The golden light of the late afternoon sun bathed them in an inviting glow. They walked among the vines, holding hands. The scent of ripening grapes filled the air. The guide's voice faded into the background as they lost themselves in their own world, savouring each other's company.

Ralph had teased her mercilessly about her inability to hold the glasses steady while flaunting her wine-tasting 'technique', her laughter ringing out as she tried—and failed repeatedly—to mimic the expert swirl she had seen the guide demonstrate.

"You will have more wine on your dress than in your glass by the end of this session", he chuckled, reaching out to catch the glass before it tipped over.

"Well, maybe if you weren't so distracting, I'd actually learn something," she shot back, pretending to pout as she wiped a few drops of wine from her dress.

He leaned in closer, his eyes twinkling with mischief. "I don't mind a little spillage—gives me an excuse to stay close to you."

She rolled her eyes, nudging him playfully with her elbow. Ralph had laughed so loud that it drew several disapproving glances from people around them.
It was one of those perfect days when the world felt like it was theirs alone.

* * *

The doorbell startled Maya. *Who could that be?* she wondered, slightly perturbed as she hurried to answer. A food parcel sat on the doorstep, accompanied by a note from her brother:

Hey, sis, I know you'd rather eat sushi alone on a Friday night than come visit me for the weekend. Sending you three boxes for the weekend, so have a great time. But seriously though, call me soon? Love, Jay

Maya chuckled. Her annoying brother, Jay, who often dropped in unexpectedly, had opted for a food delivery this time. He called weekly, acting as if he were the older sibling. Despite his antics, their bond always remained strong. But why did he assume she'd be dining solo? Had he forgotten about her husband? She went on to place the box in the refrigerator. As she turned to leave the kitchen, she was halted by a persistent beeping.

Her medication reminder on the kitchen counter had started its shrill alarm. Sighing at her forgetfulness, she grabbed the medicine box from the fridge. She was supposed to take it three hours ago—her eyes widened as she realized just how much time had slipped by. This wasn't the first time she'd lost track of something so important. Her hands trembled slightly as she fumbled with the lid, the anxiety of her own instability gnawing at the edges of her mind.

Her gaze shifted to their wedding photo on the coffee table, adorned with white lilies. An unsettling mixture of nostalgia and unease flooded her at once, and she couldn't quite grasp why, as she picked up the picture. Their glowing smiles, animated expressions, and vigorous dance poses captured the essence of their 'east meets west' wedding, all in a single frame.

Her family had spared no expense for the lavish celebration, owing to her roots. The grandeur of the Indian wedding festivities amazed Ralph's family, who had never seen celebrations on such a scale before. The vibrant colours, upbeat music, and rich traditions left them in awe. Back home, they held an intimate church ceremony with close friends and family that was equally joyful, filled with heartfelt vows and quiet moments of connection. The week-long celebration was a whirlwind of joy and excitement, but it was cut short by Ralph's work commitments. They had no choice but to postpone their grand honeymoon, promising each other they would make up for it later.

The memory of those joyous days played in Maya's mind as she tiptoed into the bathroom, clutching the bottle. Somehow, the warmth and laughter of their wedding seemed like a distant dream now, one that she longed to hold onto as her heart pounded at the sight of water overflowing from the tub. Her breath caught as she ran to close the tap, the sound of rushing water echoing in the small space.

She looked up, her eyes meeting Ralph's disapproving gaze, but before she could feel any frustration, his familiar grin appeared.

"I was just keeping it warm for you," he said, his charm instantly melting her bother.

Maya couldn't help but smile back, all her worries easing as the memories of their love and laughter intertwined with the present moment. The bathroom was filled with the scent of lavender and the soft glow of candlelight.

"Sorry, I was delayed by an unexpected email. You know Anna–" she explained.

"No problem, love. I could wait a lifetime for you," he replied, his eyes sparkling.

While flattered, a part of her was sceptical. "Sweetheart, I doubt I'd still be here if you waited a lifetime. Some other lucky woman would have you wrapped around her finger."
Ralph was undeniably attractive; his profession as a doctor added an extra layer of allure.

"Speaking of waiting, we've waited long enough to open this bottle, yeah?," he said, breaking the active banter.
Nodding, she expertly extracted the cork, and poured the crimson liquid into two glasses. The ease

with which she handled the bottle was deceiving; opening a bottle of wine was a rare skill.

"Careful, don't spill it on you," she giggled, placing the glasses on the floor before snuggling into his embrace.

"Couldn't be as embarrassing as that time you spilled wine on my shirt."

The memory of their Bordeaux mishap sent them both into fits of laughter. The sight of the deep red stain spread across his crisp white shirt was still vivid in her mind. The startled onlookers had gasped, fumbling with napkins in a futile attempt to clean it up. The embarrassment of that moment, coupled with Ralph's exaggeratedly serious expression as he tried to play it off, only made the situation more hilarious in hindsight.

"That drive home was a nightmare. I take full responsibility," she confessed.

"You have to, *mon amour*", Ralph teased, pulling her closer.

Their laughter slowly subsided. Maya was nestled against his arms, feeling a profound sense of peace. The warmth of the bathwater, combined with Ralph's steady heartbeat, lulled her into a deep slumber. Her breathing became slow and rhythmic, the day's worries dissolving into the soothing embrace of that moment.

As she slept, her dreams took her back to a peaceful vineyard bathed in clear blue sky. She felt carefree and light, running through the rows of grapevines with Ralph by her side. The sun warmed her skin, and the sweet, heady aroma of the grapes danced on the gentle breeze. Laughter filled the air as they playfully chased each other, the world around them dissolving into a perfect, timeless moment of joy.
As she drifted deeper into her dream, the vineyard seemed to stretch endlessly before them, each step bringing them closer to a horizon that promised endless happiness. The warmth of Ralph's hand in hers grounded her in the serenity of the moment. She thought her world was perfect, too perfect.

Then slowly, an unsettling feeling began to creep in, a distant, almost imperceptible hum that grew louder with each heartbeat. The colours of the vineyard started to blur, and the sun's gentle warmth grew into a searing glare, its rays stabbing at her eyes. Her grip on Ralph's hand tightened as the idyllic scene around them began to darken.
All of a sudden, the dream shifted. The hum grew closer and escalated into a deafening roar, and her peaceful dreamscape was shattered by a piercing noise. An intense beam of light flashed across her face, blinding her just as Ralph extended his arms to shield her from something unseen. And then, the tyres screeched, followed by the sharp sound of

glass shattering into countless pieces. The tranquil world she had been lost in was violently ripped away all at once.

The last thing she felt was the raw force of metal crashing against the arm that held her. A loud, gut-wrenching groan echoed through the violent impact, exploding in her ears and drowning out her world completely until she felt nothing at all.

Consciousness receded like a tide pulling back from the shore, leaving Maya adrift in a void. Darkness enveloped her, swallowing her and suffocating her until the world contracted and extinguished altogether. Then, suddenly, she was yanked back to reality.

Maya jerked awake, gasping for air, as she emerged from the water. Her body was trembling uncontrollably in the bathtub and she realised she had been in a nightmare. The transition from the peaceful dream to her harsh reality was jarring, leaving her disoriented and breathless.

Shaking and coughing uncontrollably, she held the edge of the tub, trying to pull herself upright. Maya's heart raced as she tried to steady her breathing, her mind struggling to piece together what had just happened. Her breath steadied as her eyes locked onto the floor. There, on the bathroom floor, were pieces of glass sparkling in a puddle of red wine that had spilt from her hand.

The vividness of the dream began to fade, replaced by the cold reality of her surroundings. Her fingers trembled as she touched the side of the tub, trying to soothe the cold emptiness she felt inside, with the warmth of the water.

Maya's phone buzzed, jolting her further awake, but she was too stunned to answer. The sound was distant, almost unreal, as if coming from another world. Slowly, in the silence of the bathroom, the solitary echo of her own breath forced her to face the truth–she was alone in the tub. She had been, all this time.
There was no Ralph.

Maya reached for her phone with trembling fingers, clutching it tightly as if to anchor herself to the real world. A few seconds later, a voice note popped up from her mother. Maya reluctantly pressed play. Her mother's voice came in worried and rushed -

Hi my dear, I called you twice. Please call me back immediately. Also, did you schedule your next appointment with Doctor Stephanie? I hope you are taking your pills regularly. She keeps stressing how important it is at this stage of your treatment. Did Jay call you ? He sent some food over, so you won't have to worry about cooking. I know it is no fun cooking alone… we all worry about you. Your dad says hi too, he's just gone out for….

And then, it hit her. Maya wanted to coil up inside the tub, wishing the water would drown out her world again. The nightmare was over, but the reality was far worse. She was left to face it alone.

Without Ralph. Her mind had played its cruel tricks again, offering her a fleeting illusion, only to snatch it away.

Staring at the red-steaked floor, a bitter laugh escaped her lips as she picked up the wine bottle and thought, *At least this time I will be able to wipe the stain off.* The thought was hollow, a flimsy attempt to find some semblance of control in a moment that felt as shattered as the pieces of glass around her.
"No Ralph," she whispered, the words slowly sinking in, reverberating through the emptiness of the room. The silence felt like a living thing, pressing in on her from all sides and wrapping around her like a vice.
She closed her eyes, desperate to escape, hoping to fall asleep once more or plunge back into the darkness. But no matter how hard she tried, her mind kept replaying the horrific car accident that had taken her Ralph away from her forever, leaving behind a void that could never be filled. The memories kept playing on an endless loop, each one serving only to deepen the despair that had seeped into her bones. And the shadows were growing, creeping closer, smashing her under their weight.
Unable to suffer, she switched off the light and gulped down the wine in the dark, the liquid burning her throat as she whispered, "No Ralph." over and over. The words hung in the air like a haunting reminder of her shattered world until, they pulled her deeper into the darkness, where she finally hid from the reality she could no longer bear to face.

The bridesmaid's secret

Freedom blooms beneath forgiveness

"You should have seen the dress, Liz. It was this beautiful blush pink with lace detailing. Absolutely magical!"

Elizabeth adjusted her glasses and glanced at her friend, Sophie, who was sighing dreamily over another weekend wedding. She looked more lovestruck than the bride. Placing the coffee cup on her desk, Liz marvelled at how Sophie could radiate sunshine at eight in the morning while she was barely awake.

"Got any pictures?" Liz asked, hoping that might wake her up.

Sophie flung her chair back, rushing over to Liz's desk. She plopped down with a thud and scrolled through her phone's photo gallery with the speed of a hummingbird while Liz's gaze darted to the precariously balanced coffee cup on the table. A coffee stain on the desk was bad enough, but imagine the horror of a morning coffee shower!

Sophie had always adored weddings. As a little girl, she'd spend hours flipping through bridal magazines, dreaming of wedding dresses and happily-ever-afters. Her room was filled with romance novels and DVDs of rom-coms growing up. While she lived in a world painted with vibrant hues and fairy tales, Liz preferred the monochrome shades of logic and practicality. She often marvelled at how their friendship had thrived over the years. Sporty and passionately left-brained, Liz was an avid gamer who landed her dream job right out of college. She thrived in the city, where she translated her logical thinking into creating immersive digital experiences as a game developer.

About a year ago, Sophie reached out to her, seeking a job, and happily accepted an offer as a content writer at the same company. She was thrilled about moving back to the city because it meant having a more vibrant social circle and access to a larger dating pool.

With her infectious laughter and open-hearted nature, she effortlessly connected with a diverse group of people, from artists to entrepreneurs. She became close friends with Samara, a PR executive who enjoyed all the finest things urban living had to offer.

One day, Samara called her, feeling under the weather with the flu.

"Soph, it's terrible! I couldn't get out of bed all day. How will I go to Cancún? Tammy's already freaking out that one of her bridesmaids is going to be a no-show. She said it's a bad sign," Samara sniffed over the phone.

"The sunshine would do you good," Sophie paused. "Wait... the wedding is in Cancún?" Her eyes enlarged.

Samara could sense her expression even over a voice call.

"Yes, destination wedding. Umm.. I have an idea. Why don't you go in my place as a bridesmaid? You'll love it. I know you love weddings, too," she suggested, giggling slightly.

"Gosh, I'd love to, but.."

"..but what? It's done then. I'll call Tammy right away and text you the details."

"Sam, wait... I'm. not sure. I don't know anybody."

"Don't worry, I hardly know anyone except the bride, who is an ex-client."

Sophie believed her. She hesitated but then thought of the adventure and agreed. Maybe this was exactly what she needed.

"And hey, Soph, would you mind picking up a few stuff for me while you're there…"

But Sophie was barely listening. Her thoughts were already drifting towards bridesmaid dresses, and a surge of excitement ran through her like a heat wave.

It turned out that Sophie was a natural-born bridesmaid. She was efficient but upbeat, organized yet cheerful, and always knew how to soothe a stressed bride.

All the bridesmaids huddled together during one such wedding to address a most pressing bridal emergency.
"What will he think of me? It is our wedding, and I still haven't been able to put into words what I feel". The bride was speaking through sobs, growing hysterical by the minute. She patted her face with tissues and powder while holding a blank piece of paper. Her panic over an empty speech led to an unexpected reveal of Sophie's talent for writing heartfelt wedding speeches on the fly.
Later, once everyone had settled, the bride sat across the dinner table, mouthed, "Thank you", and drew an *'air heart'* with her fingers, smiling at Sophie.

The next day, Sophie signed up on an online 'hire-a-bridesmaid' website, embarking on a series of bridesmaid adventures. Each Monday, she regaled Liz with tales from the weekend weddings, sharing pictures and gifts and beaming with pride over her top-rated reputation. After honing her shadow-writing skills at a few more weddings, she decided to launch an online service to offer her speech-writing talent to a broader audience.

"Besides, it will be a little extra money for my romantic honeymoon in Mykonos.", Sophie told Liz the day her website went live.

Liz looked sympathetic, but only for a moment.

"Yeah, yeah, I know. So what if I haven't found him yet? I will someday.. soon," Sophie said, looking out the window, ignoring the notification from her dating app.
For all her outward optimism about her love life, Sophie was terrified. She often scheduled dates with matches only to cancel at the last minute.

"How long are you going to do this?" Liz would ask bluntly in an attempt to confront her friend about her dating fears. Perhaps Sophie was afraid of disappointment, but she couldn't say for sure.

Sophie watched in awe as her online business flourished, fueled by the connections she had made at countless weddings. Clients raved about her heartfelt speeches, and soon, her inbox flooded with requests from all over the world. One day, an email from an unfamiliar sender stood out among the rest. It read -

> *"Dear Ms. Sophie,*
>
> *I am contacting you on behalf of Mr. Parker. He is getting married soon and would like your help with his wedding speech. We've heard excellent things about your work. Please let us know if you're available.*
>
> *Best regards, Lila."*

Sophie's heart skipped a beat. *It could not be!*

She frantically typed the address mentioned at the bottom of the email. Her eyes scanned the screen as she scoured the internet for every detail about Liam Parker. To her horror, it was indeed the same Liam from high school. He had been living in the same city for the past five years, and the office address in the email was a few buildings away from hers. He was a high-powered executive who-.

Sophie stopped and closed her eyes, exhaling deeply. She had always known Liam would become wealthy and successful. The realization that their lives had turned out exactly as they had once envisioned brought a sting of disappointment, almost bringing her to tears. Liam, her high school sweetheart, had ended things with her over an abrupt text on the night of their graduation.

Devastated, Sophie locked herself away in her room for eight days. No one, not even Liz, could reach her until one evening when she stormed into Sophie's room, threatening to end their friendship if Sophie didn't snap out of it.

She hadn't seen him since high school, but she had never forgotten him nor forgiven him.

"Liz," she said the next day, her voice trembling. "Guess who just contacted me about a wedding speech."

"Who?"

"Liam Parker."

Liz's eyes widened on her usually expressionless face. "Liam? As in your high school Liam? Wow, that's... unexpected."

An uneasy silence passed by.

"He reached out to you himself?" Liz asked.

"No, it was his assistant who contacted me. He doesn't know about it yet."

"So, are you going to do it?"

"I don't know."

Sophie's mind raced. Unsure if she should accept the request, she hurried out for a walk. Liz stared behind her. She returned after an hour and announced, "It's okay, I'm a professional. I will do it."

She wouldn't let her personal feelings interfere with her work, so she agreed to write the speech. After all, it had all happened a long time ago.

But as soon as she started writing the speech, memories came flooding back to her like a river in full flow - the promises they had made to each other, the dreams they had shared. Each word she wrote felt like peeling back a layer of her heart, exposing old wounds she thought had been forgotten. After finishing it, she reread the speech and realized it might be her best yet.

A month later, Sophie sat at her office desk, deeply absorbed in her latest project. Suddenly, she noticed a tall figure in a tailored suit walk through the front door. Recognizing who it was, she stood up, smoothed her skirt, and braced herself to face him.

"Liam?" her voice sounded calm even though her heart was pounding, "What are you doing here?"

"Hi, Sophie." The sunlight caught the chiselled features of his clean-shaven face as his mouth curved into a warm smile, barely revealing a set of perfectly white teeth. Except for the slight crinkle at the corners of his eyes, which added a touch of sincerity to his expression, he looked almost unchanged after all these years.

"I tried to email you. *Twice*. But never got a response."

It was true. Sophie had received an email from him about a week after his wedding -

> *"Dear Sophie,*
>
> *I found out you wrote my wedding speech. Can we meet? There's so much I want to say.*
>
> *Best,*
>
> *Liam"*

And then again, a week later -

"Hey Sophie,

I know you are in the same city. Can we please just meet once?

-Liam"

Yes, she had intentionally ignored his emails, and although the urge to respond had lingered for a while, she was content to let bygones be bygones. *What was there to say? Why would he want to dredge up the past?*

"Sophie", Liam continued, "I found out from Lila that you wrote my speech. It was beautiful. But seeing those words…" he paused, "I just needed to see you."

"How did you find out I work here?" Sophie asked, crossing her arms.

"That wasn't too hard to figure out" this time, he grinned.

"Look, Soph, can we talk? For a bit? There's a coffee shop around the corner.."

Sophie hesitated at first but then, agreed.

They entered the coffee shop and ordered their drinks, exchanging polite smiles with the barista, though the tension between them was unmistakable.

Once seated, Liam fidgeted with his cup, his eyes darting around the room as if searching for the right words. He began, "Sophie, I owe you an apology. I shouldn't have ended things the way I did. It was cowardly and wrong."

The hum of the coffee shop filled the space between them. Liam took a slow sip of his coffee, his gaze steady on Sophie, who stared out the window, tracing the rim of her cup with her fingers.
Finally, Sophie broke the silence, her voice soft but firm. "It hurt, Liam. A lot."

Liam nodded, his expression serious. The pain in her voice was still evident.
"I know, Sophie. I've thought about it every day since. The truth is, I didn't fare as well in my high school exams, and that shook me. I started doubting myself, questioning everything. I was scared I wouldn't be able to live up to the promises we made, that I'd drag you down with me."

Sophie turned to face him, a look of consternation on her face as her eyes searched his. "But why didn't you discuss what was on your mind with me? Instead, you just disappeared. One moment, we were talking about the future, about everything we wanted to do together, and then... nothing. A text. That's all I got."
Liam swallowed, guilt shadowing his features. "I didn't know how to face you. The fear of failing, of not being good enough, consumed me. So, I took the

coward's way out, thinking it would be easier for both of us if I ended it quickly. But it wasn't. It was just cruel."

He paused to read her expression, but Sophie looked down at her cup. He continued, sounding even more remorseful. "I saw Liz outside your building a few months back... she didn't notice me - but I wanted to go up and ask her about your whereabouts. Something stopped me that day. I wasn't sure if I could face you. And then, the wedding happened and…", he broke off.

She was staring at her cup, her fingers coming to a still when she spoke. "For a long time, I wondered what I did wrong, why you didn't talk to me. I replayed that night over and over in my head, trying to understand. But all I found was more questions, more hurt."

Liam leaned forward, his voice earnest. "Sophie, you did nothing wrong. It was all on me. I was overwhelmed by the thought of everything changing after graduation, of us moving in different directions. I didn't have the courage to admit I was scared, so I ran. And I've regretted it ever since."

Sophie blinked, trying to hold back her tears. She steadied her voice before speaking again. "Sitting here with you, I realize I've been holding onto something that no longer serves me. I've moved on in so many ways, yet I've let this one thing stay, keeping me from truly letting go."

With a mix of admiration and remorse in his eyes, Liam watched her. "I'm so sorry, Sophie. I know I can't change what I did, but I want you to know that you deserved so much better than how I treated you."

Sophie nodded, feeling the weight of his words settle into her heart. "Writing that speech for your wedding...it stirred up so much, but it also helped me start letting go. Seeing you now, hearing you say these things, it's like the final piece of the puzzle."

Slowly, Liam smiled. He reached across the table, his hand hovering before gently placing it over hers. "Soph? I mean it. You deserve better."

Her heart swelled at his words, warmth spreading through her—perhaps, it was the warmth of closure, she thought.

"Thank you, Liam. Thank you for coming to see me today."

They sat in silence for a few more moments. The tension between them gradually melted away, and soon, the conversation flowed naturally. They found themselves reminiscing about their high school days, laughing while recalling late-night study sessions, sneaking out to watch movies, and exchanging secret notes in class. The years seemed to fall away as they spoke about college, jobs, and how life had, indeed, taken them on very different paths.

When the time came to leave, they stood and nodded, agreeing to part as friends now that the weight of the past had finally lifted from their shoulders.

Sophie felt lighter, her resentment replaced by a sense of closure. For the first time in years, her heart was open to new possibilities. Allowing that feeling to linger for a while longer, she waved Liam goodbye and walked back to the office at a leisurely pace.

When Sophie entered the office, her phone buzzed with a notification. Curious, she pulled it out of her pocket and read the message, an amused smile touching her face: *You have a new match.* She held her smile for a moment too long, then glanced up, searching for Liz. Across the room, their eyes met, and Liz winked, with a thumbs-up. Somehow, no words were needed—Liz always knew. And yet, Sophie had always considered herself the know-it-all.

Chuckling, Sophie turned and walked back to her desk, where a picture of Mykonos still hung prominently as a symbol of her hopeful future.

A New Chapter

Beyond the shadows of the past

The morning sunlight streaming through the curtains provided Ajay with ample brightness as he bent over to tie his shoelaces, ready to step out of his house.
His fingers froze mid-loop when he heard a sharp scream followed by the sound of glass hitting the floor. Heart pounding against his chest, he ran to the bedroom with half-tied laces. For a moment, he paused and listened for any further sounds outside the door before pushing it open.

His heart was in his throat when he found her sprawled naked across the bathroom floor, a dark stain of blood seeping out of one hand while trying to prop herself up with the other in an attempt to rise up. He stared at her, immobilised by a thousand thoughts crossing his mind. *Had she again?*
Her terrified eyes held him for a second when he knelt beside her before moving up to the broken clamp stand, shards of glass spread under it. Relief washed over him after realising it was not what he had feared.

"I slipped", Kavya muttered.
And dragged down the glass stand with her, Ajay concluded, looking at the resulting wound that had pierced into her right palm.
He rushed to hand her the towel, and she quickly enveloped herself in it, shuddering as her senses kicked back in.

"We have to go to the hospital immediately. I will grab some bandages from the kitchen."

Ajay frantically searched through the kitchen drawers. *Where did she keep it?* The humid Kolkata weather had already dampened his shirt. It's better to call in sick today, he thought, reaching into the chestnut brown cabinet above the sink and finally seizing the kit. He never quite understood why his wife stored things in less height-accessible places. The kitchen sink was laden with unwashed vessels from the previous day, including his coffee mug from earlier this morning, which he ignored and ran back to the room.

Kavya stood outside the bathroom door, still wrapped in the towel he'd given her, cupping the wound with her other hand to prevent blood from dripping to the floor. Ajay winced on her behalf while applying antiseptic over it and wrapping the bandage firmly around her hand. He *always* disliked blood.

"Do we have to go to the hospital? This looks secure enough", Kavya asked apprehensively, unable to meet his eye.

"We do"

They drove to the hospital in silence. Kavya was adrift in her thoughts, gazing out the window at the spirited morning rush, a kind of chaotic energy that could only be found in the city of joy - roads dense with all sorts of transportation, hawkers peddling their carts amidst countless vehicles, two-wheelers zigzagging through crowded roads much to the disgust of passengers in yellow ambassador taxis.

Wires crisscrossed above them under a sky that was barely visible while the occasional outbursts of *rickshaw walas* added to the barbaric July heat like spices sizzling in hot oil.

They drove past their favourite sweet shop, where a familiar face at the counter was rolling soft rasgulla balls clad in a white vest that barely covered his paunch. He stood behind a large vessel, smirking at the tempted passersby as he dipped the spongy balls into a glistening syrup.

Kavya watched people throng the sidewalks, their figures blurring against the backdrop of discoloured buildings with colourful signboards written in Bengali, train tracks embedded in the thoroughfare, and run-down colonial buildings with broken windows and washed-off paint.

Ajay rubbed the sweat from his forehead after stopping at a signal after stopping at a signal, feeling his body itch. He glanced at Kavya, baffled at how unruffled she was, quietly absorbed in the world of activities outside. He had not turned on the car's air conditioning, and she did not seem to bother either. She didn't bother about these things anymore. She had stopped bothering about stuff for a long time now.

Ajay's thoughts trailed back to when their conversations filled the car before the silence took over. It was only a year ago when their car rides were regularly punctuated by heated arguments about the AC:

"Can't you just roll down the windows? It's not that hot, and we are stuck in traffic anyway"

To which she would retort, "And invite the whole city's dust and pollution inside? You would rather I choke my lungs than burn your fuel.", her big, round, kohl-rimmed eyes turning into thunderclouds.

Ajay had rolled his eyes at her and said, "Tch, don't be dramatic. Think about the people outside. Are they not alive?"

"Fine, fine. You are the one who has to pay the bills for my allergy medications and doctor visits!"

She slumped back into her seat, arms crossed.

Ajay cracked into laughter and turned to her, holding up her chin, "I have a better plan, shona. How about I pay the bill for our dinner date at the Taj this Sunday?"

Kavya turned and squealed with joy, hugging him in an instant. Then, she quickly retracted after noticing the stares of passengers from nearby vehicles.

Although thriftiness was one of Ajay's strongest virtues, he never let it prevent him from pampering his beloved wife.

"So, will you wear that new saree I gifted you?"

Kavya nodded, quickly turning toward the window to hide her blushing face—the same face she had that morning after seeing the sheer red saree he had wrapped for her with a red rose.

Their second wedding anniversary was a special one, filled with anticipation of things to welcome in the coming months.

Little did they know that their lives and their marriage would turn upside down in a mere two months. Now, living as strangers under the same roof, their laughter-filled days were just ghosts of the past, filling the space between them.

The pervasive scent of antiseptic hanging in the air mingled with distant echoes of emergencies that were constantly in and out of sight as they walked down the hospital corridors to their allotted chamber.

Kavya winced in pain when the doctor unwrapped the bandage to examine her hand, the only noticeable expression on her detached pallor. Ajay was staring at the stark white of the walls, trying hard to focus on the present medical concern while fighting the tide of emotions washing over him after they'd crossed *the room*. At once, he regretted his decision to bring her to this hospital, remembering the tragedy that had unfolded within its walls and crushed them less than a year ago.

At least her wound would heal this time, he thought ruefully. His face suddenly clouded with an inexplicable sorrow darkening his pupils. He turned away and quietly exited the room. Kavya's eyes had seen his.

Fortunately, her wound healed within five days, as the glass had not penetrated too deeply into the tissues. On the sixth day, Ajay came home to an unexpected surprise waiting in the kitchen.
Kavya stood beside the gas stove, her body quivering slightly when she saw him walk in.

"Made aloo *posto*", she muttered softly.

She sat across from him at the table, having served him a plate of rice, dal, his favourite potato dish, and a piece of deep-fried fish. They dined in silence, looking up from their plates only once to pass the dal. His gaze lingered on her under the soft yellow glow of the dining light, noticing the dark circles hollowing her eyes. Her frame was thin, and she looked much older than her age—fragile, exhausted. Yet, there was an undeniable beauty about her, a delicate, vulnerable glow that seemed to emerge from a grief he knew all too well.
He had watched helplessly as she spiralled into self-destruction, denial, and self-imposed isolation after that tragic event. Initially, she lashed out in anger, hurling accusations at him.

"You weren't even there," she had said the day he found her lying on the kitchen floor, bleeding from her wrist. Horrified, Ajay rushed her to the hospital.

After a few similar incidents, she suddenly retreated into silence. The more he tried to reach out, the deeper she buried herself. Her defence mechanisms had inadvertently built walls around them.
Ajay ached to speak to her, to bridge the widening gap between them. Nights found him staring at the empty side of their bed, his heart heavy with the weight of unexpressed sorrow. He longed to hear her voice, to share his own pain and fears.

In those quiet moments, he would rehearse conversations in his mind, imagining the words that might break through her silence. But each morning, he faced the same unyielding barriers.
Consumed by his despair and loneliness, Ajay sought refuge in work, his days blurring into a series of tasks and deadlines in a desperate attempt to drown out their loss.

But that night, as they sat together after a long time, having dinner, the silence between them was no longer heavy with unspoken words but filled with tentative hope. His gentle gaze met hers, and for the first time in months, she didn't look away. It was only a fleeting moment, but it felt significant—a sign that perhaps, finally, their hearts were beginning to heal.

The next day, Ajay left early from office. He steered his car towards the neighbourhood park just before reaching his street. Stepping out, he craned his neck to see through the greenery for any recognisable faces meandering inside. He and Kavya had walked here every evening until eight months ago.

They would talk for hours, hand-in-hand beneath the tall trees, making plans to decorate their home with plants and the pitter-patter of little feet. He settled onto the same bench where he had often shared stories about his work and colleagues while Kavya listened intently, crunching noisily on a packet of *nimkis*.

The slight rustle of a nearby bush diverted his thoughts, and a sudden presence caught him off guard. His heart skipped a beat when the silhouette stood still for a moment.

Kavya emerged silently from behind a tree. She looked at him for a long second before sitting down beside him.

"Did you know I would be here?" he enquired, glancing sideways at her.

"Maybe"

They sat in silence, watching the children laughing near the see-saws as one of the parents chided them. A ball rolled to a stop at Ajay's feet. Behind it, a little boy came running, accompanied by a tiny dog woofing alongside him.

Ajay smiled and tried to playfully keep the ball from the boy, struggling to push it behind his legs. The boy burst into giggles at Ajay's antics. Ajay picked up the ball with a gentle smile and tossed it back to the boy, who caught it in one leap. Grinning widely, the boy exclaimed, "Thank you!" before racing his dog back to the play area.

Ajay watched them go, a wave of emotions stirring deep within him. Unable to hold them back, he looked down at the ground and burst into tears.

After a few moments, Kavya leaned closer, resting her hand on his shoulder.

"Ajay," she whispered softly, her voice filled with concern.

He pressed the bench with his hands for additional support, choking back sobs. "It hasn't been easy for me at all," he said, his voice trembling. "I know you blame me, but…" His words trailed off as he continued to look down.

Kavya turned to him, her eyes searching his face. "Blame you for what?"

"For not being there", Ajay replied, his voice barely above a whisper.

"You *were* there," Kavya said softly, her hand gently squeezing his shoulder.

"Yes, but not when it happened", Ajay said, his voice breaking.

Kavya took a deep breath, her voice trembling when she spoke. "We both lost so much that day, Ajay.

But blaming ourselves or each other won't help. We need to find a way to heal together."

At that moment, Ajay looked up to meet her gaze for the first time, seeing a glimmer of the connection they once shared.

The birds were retreating now, their distant chirping fading into the background, echoing the day's end. Kavya closed her eyes, slowly looking up at the sky. "I know he is out there somewhere, playing, probably chasing butterflies, happy. Our little one."

When she turned to look back at him, her eyes became moist with tears. A soft, serene smile touched her pale face, its growing curvature a testament to an inner peace that had begun to radiate outward.

She pressed his cheek and said, "I am sorry for everything, Ajay."

"So am I." Ajay bent to her side and held her other hand, the same one that had been injured and is now healed.

They remained seated in the park long after the sun had set and no other souls were in sight, sobbing silently in the darkness.

The following morning, Ajay stirred awake in bed to the rhythmic sounds of vessels clinking and the steady flow of water running from the kitchen tap.

He sat up slowly, rubbing his eyes, and noticed a neatly folded note on his bedside table, pinned down by his reading glasses. With a mix of interest and apprehension, he reached over and picked it up.

As he unfolded the note, he immediately recognised the handwriting before reading the first word.

Can we start a new chapter? It read.

Ajay studied the note for a long moment, a slow smile spreading across his face as he made his way into the kitchen to greet his wife.

Dance your heart away

Step up

The projector hummed to life, casting a sharp, rectangular glow on the pristine white wall of Avantech Solutions' largest conference room. One by one, the room filled with attendees, the key players finding their designated seats with practised ease.

Dhruv stood next to the projector, his sharp eyes scanning the room as he prepared to lead the quarterly business review. The bold, stark figures projected on the screen were his domain. As Head of Revenue for the Asia-Pacific region, his confidence was unmistakable. He led the discussion with ease, swiftly answering every question from the stakeholders. As he delved into the quarter's earnings and deals, his words sliced through the data like a surgeon's scalpel, turning complex figures into clear insights.

At the far end of the imposing room, Bhavna sat quietly, diligently taking notes. A mere two months into her internship, the corporate world was still a jungle to her and a far cry from the university lecture halls she was used to. Dhruv was a towering figure in her professional landscape.

Despite his intimidating presence, she couldn't help but admire his poise and command of the room, a stark contrast to her own self-doubt.

The meeting concluded, and Bhavna made her way to the water cooler. Her colleague, Ananya, greeted her with a teasing smile. "So, rookie, how'd it go?"

Bhavna's eyes sparkled with admiration. "Dhruv is so charismatic", she gushed. "How does he *always* handle everything so effortlessly?"
Ananya chuckled. "Dhruv has been here for over a decade. He's not only closed some of our biggest deals but also turned around failing projects. He's practically a legend here."
"I can see that..."
"By the way, did you know he joined as an intern, too? Just like you."

Bhavna almost squirmed at the thought of the immense expectations that awaited her. "I wish I could be more like him. I messed up a client demo last week; my manager let me have it. I felt I let her down."
Ananya's expression softened.
She had walked this path herself and knew the struggles a greenhorn like Bhavna would encounter. Placing a comforting hand on her shoulder, she said, "It's okay, we all make mistakes, Bhavna. Don't be so hard on yourself. Just learn from it and move on."
Bhavna nodded.

"And if you need anything, you know whom to call" Ananya winked and headed back to her desk. Bhavna watched her walk away with a smile. She was one of the few people who made the office bearable, and Bhavna often thanked her lucky stars for Ananya's existence.

As the day dragged on, Bhavna's internal struggle deepened. The shadow of her manager's disappointment hung heavy over her, amplifying the isolation she felt among her fellow interns. Each passing hour seemed to add weight to her already heavy burden, and the pressure to prove herself became suffocating. It was as if, despite her best efforts, she couldn't shake off that gnawing feeling of inadequacy. But as the clock ticked closer to the end of the workday, a spark of energy ignited within her. It was time for her dance class, a much-needed escape from the confines of the office.

Arriving at the dance studio, Bhavna's transformation was immediate. As soon as she slipped into her dancing shoes, the shy, uncertain intern was replaced by a poised and graceful dancer. Her movements were as fluid as water, dissolving her worries with each step. This was her special place, and she could always turn to it whenever needed.

By the end of the session, her confidence had returned. As she straightened up to grab her bag, ready to exit the studio, she collided with a tall figure, nearly toppling over.

"Dhruv?" she exclaimed, her eyes wide with surprise and disbelief.

He stepped back, taking a moment to recognize her. "Uh, yeah, you're... the intern, right?" he stammered, his awkwardness palpable.

Of course, he does not know my name. Bhavna almost winced at her foolishness. "Yes, I'm Bhavna."
Dhruv seemed to be gathering his thoughts. "Are you okay?" he asked, remembering their collision and looking distracted.
"Yeah, I'm fine," Bhavna said, nodding vigorously.
A few silent seconds passed by.
"I didn't know you danced," she offered, trying to fill the awkward moment.
He seemed caught off guard. "Neither did I about you. Uh... I'm late for my class. See you at the office?"

Feeling flustered, she watched him go after his brief, almost dismissive wave. She couldn't decide if she was more furious or embarrassed.

The next day, they found themselves in class during the same time slot. Still unnerved by the previous day's encounter, Bhavna pretended to focus intently on her dance, avoiding any eye contact with Dhruv. As the class ended, she gathered her things, hoping to slip away unnoticed. But Dhruv approached her with the same air of confidence as if he were walking into a boardroom.
"Hey, Bhavna," he began, his voice sincere. I'm sorry about yesterday. I didn't expect to see someone from the office, and I was just... a *little* surprised." His face grimaced at 'little'.
Bhavna managed a small smile. "It's okay, I understand. I never expected to see anyone from work here either."

Dhruv nodded, relief evident in his expression. "I guess we both have our secret escapes. Dance is my way of de-stressing from the office madness."
Bhavna's curiosity was piqued. "Really? I wouldn't have guessed. You always seem so in control."
Dhruv chuckled. "Appearances can be deceiving. Work can be pretty intense sometimes, and this is my way of letting loose."
Bhavna nodded in understanding. 'Dance is not just my escape but my passion too. It's where I feel most like myself.' She relaxed, finding common ground.

Dhruv looked at her with renewed interest. "You're really good. How long have you been dancing?"
"Since I was a kid," Bhavna admitted, a glint of pride in her eyes. I've always loved it," she said, then her voice changed. " But it's hard to balance with work and..."
Dhruv noticed the hesitation on her face and arched his eyebrows, inquiring softly.
"And responsibilities, I meant", she forced a half-smile.
Dhruv nodded thoughtfully and said, "I get that. It's a challenge, but it's worth it. Maybe we can help each other out. Keep each other motivated?"
Bhavna's smile grew. "That would be great!"
"Agreed," Dhruv replied with genuine warmth in his voice. "See you in the next class?"

As Bhavna watched him disappear from her view, her heart pounded in her chest. Over the next few days, Bhavna found herself looking forward to seeing him at the studio. What started as casual encounters in the dance studio began to feel like something more, leaving her both surprised and curious. How could she, so unlike him, feel such a strange but comforting connection? Yet, here it was, undeniably real, unfolding quietly and naturally.

As the weeks went by, their friendship blossomed. At Dhruv's request, Bhavna adjusted her schedule to coincide with his, and soon it became a routine for him to wait for her after every class. Their post-dance strolls to the nearby tea stall became a ritual where they could shed their corporate masks and connect on a more personal level. They chatted about the office, deadlines, projects, colleagues, and gradually, their other interests as well.

Bhavna was surprised by how easily she found herself opening up to Dhruv. Despite his imposing presence at work, he was a great listener—patient, attentive, and surprisingly empathetic. She felt at ease sharing details about her life that she rarely discussed with anyone else. She confided in him her dream of opening a dance studio.

However, she admitted that her financial responsibilities as the sole breadwinner of her family made it impossible for her to pursue it at the moment.

Dhruv, in turn, revealed a side of himself that few at the office knew. He spoke of the frustrations and pressures of his high-flying job, which, despite its outward glamour, left him feeling empty and unfulfilled. "Sometimes, I wonder if it's all worth it," he confessed one evening, his voice tinged with weariness as he sipped his hot *kulhad* tea.

One evening, after practice, they found themselves at their usual spot at the tea stall, the comforting aroma of spiced chai wrapping around them.

Dhruv leaned back in his chair, a teasing grin on his lips. "So, how's office life treating you as a full-time employee now? Still messing up those demos?" he joked, his tone light but his eyes warm.

Bhavna's face flushed a deep shade of red, the playful jab striking a chord she hadn't expected. Dhruv quickly noticed the change in her demeanour, his grin fading as he sensed something was off. She hesitated, her fingers fidgeting with the rim of her cup until she finally spoke, "Dhruv, there's something I need to tell you," she began, her voice laced with nervousness. "I received an offer from another company."

Dhruv's smile disappeared, replaced by an unreadable expression. His gaze locked onto hers, searching for something she couldn't quite place. After what felt like an eternity, he finally spoke, his voice steady but cautious. "So, what are you thinking? Have you accepted it?"

"I'm not sure yet," Bhavna admitted, her voice barely above a whisper as she cast her eyes downward. "It's a good opportunity, financially. But..." Her words trailed off, the weight of her uncertainty hanging between them.

Dhruv leaned forward, his usual playful demeanour replaced by an intensity that caught her off guard. "But?" he urged gently,

Dhruv leaned forward, his attention focused on her. "But?" his voice filled with a quiet urgency.

Bhavna took a deep breath, struggling to put her feelings into words. "I'm not sure if leaving is the right decision," she confessed, her vulnerability laid bare.

Her eyes searched his face, hoping for some answers or signs of reassurance, but his expression remained inscrutable.

The silence that followed felt heavy. A wave of regret washed over her. What if she had made a mistake by confiding in him? What if he used this against her? The thought sent a shiver down her spine. They sipped their drinks in silence, the unspoken tension between them palpable, each lost in their own thoughts as the evening air grew cooler around them.

After their conversation, Bhavna couldn't shake the uneasy feeling that had settled in her chest. Dhruv's unexpected absence the following week made it worse. Each time she entered the studio, she half-expected to see him there, waiting with his easy smile, but he never appeared. Her anxiety grew with each passing day. At the office, his absence was just as conspicuous. Every time she walked by his cabin, it was either empty or the door was closed for yet another meeting. The silence between them gnawed at her, and doubt began to creep in. *Had she said too much? Had she made a mistake in trusting him?*

The uncertainty weighed heavily on her; it was all she could think about as the days stretched. Finally, just when the tension had reached its peak, Dhruv approached her desk. His serious expression sent a jolt of unease through her.

"Bhavna, can we talk?" he asked, his tone devoid of the usual lightness she had come to expect. Bhavna's heart raced as she followed him to a quiet corner.

"I've decided to quit my job," Dhruv said, his voice steady. "I took some time off last week to think things over. I have decided to move to the mountains for a few months and will figure it out from there." He paused, looking at her closely and allowing the words to sink in. "I know it sounds crazy, but I've thought about it for a long time. I've realized that life is too short to spend in a job that brings me no happiness. I have some investments of my own, so I'll manage." He stopped and looked into her eyes. "You should do the same, Bhavna."

Bhavna was stunned. "Dhruv, I... I don't know what to say."

Sensing the whirlwind of thoughts in her mind, he asked gently, "Have you accepted the job offer?"

"Yes, I did," Bhavna said quietly, looking down.

Dhruv looked at her with sympathy. After a few moments, he said, "I understand why you made that choice. But just promise me one thing." As she looked up to meet his gaze, he added, "You're an incredible dancer, Bhavna. Don't let that go to waste."

A swirl of emotions washed over Bhavna as she stood there, watching Dhruv disappear from sight. The realization that she might never see him again—neither at work nor in the dance studio—hit her harder than she had expected. His final words echoed in her mind long after she went home, planting the seed of a possibility she had never dared to consider.

As she lay in bed that night, her mind wandered to the mountains where Dhruv would soon find his peace. She wondered if she, too, could find her own peace by following the path her heart had long desired.

The following day, Bhavna arrived a bit earlier than usual at her dance class. Before slipping into her shoes, she took a deep breath and approached the owner and instructor, a kind woman named Anjana. "Anjana," Bhavna began, her voice trembling slightly with nervousness. "I have a request. Would it be possible for me to volunteer or work here as a part-time instructor?" Her heart pounded in her chest as she awaited Anjana's response.

'Of course, Bhavna,' Anjana replied warmly. 'We would love to have you on board.'

Bhavna's heart soared as the words flooded her senses. They were sweeter than music to her ears, filling her with a joy she hadn't felt in a long time. At that moment, she felt a deep sense of validation, as though all her dreams were finally within reach. The fear and doubt that had once held her back seemed to melt away, replaced by a bubbling excitement. She thanked Anjana with a beaming smile and, with renewed energy, put on her dancing shoes, ready to dance her way into the life she had begun to dream of once more.

The weeks that followed felt different for Bhavna. The dance studio, once a place of routine solace, now carried a possibility she couldn't shake off. Each step she took in the studio echoed Dhruv's words, urging her to pursue the life she had dreamed of. And then, one day, her phone buzzed with a message from an unknown number.

'Bhavna, it's Dhruv. I finally made it to the mountains. I've been hiking all morning. The view from my window is breathtaking. How's everything at your end?'

Bhavna smiled at the screen. She replied quickly, her fingers tapping out the words: *'Dhruv, it's so good to hear from you! Things are... different. I took your advice and started working part-time as a dance instructor. It feels incredible like I'm finally stepping into my own. And the best part is, I can do this besides my full-time job.'*

Moments later, her phone chimed again.

I'm so proud of you, Bhavna. It sounds like you're finding your rhythm. Keep at it, and who knows—maybe one day, we'll meet again, or better yet, share another dance?'

Bhavna's heart swelled with joy as she read his words. A smile played on her lips as she replied: *I'd love that, Dhruv. I'll save a dance for you—whenever you're ready.*

His response came almost immediately: *It's a date then. I'll be waiting.*

Bhavna's smile deepened as she reread his words, her fingers hovering over the screen. She hesitated, then typed: *Until then, I'll keep practising. You better be ready to keep up with me.*

Dhruv's reply was playful and light: *Challenge accepted! Just don't make me look too bad out there. Take care, Bhavna. And remember, life's a dance—sometimes, we just need to find the right partner. A few seconds later, he sent a wink.*

Bhavna's heart skipped a beat. She held her phone close, feeling a warmth that had nothing to do with the device in her hand. For the first time in a long while, she felt a flutter of anticipation, not just for her dreams but for the possibilities that awaited with Dhruv. The future felt wide open, and as she tucked her phone away, she couldn't help but imagine where this new dance might lead them both.

A Page-Turned Love

Unscripted Hearts

Background: *Suzy and Gary are both introverted bookworms, their lives steeped in the fictional worlds they adore. Real-life adventures interested them less. Meeting at a library one evening, Suzy finds herself in a panic after discovering she'd lost the book she intended to return. As the librarian's patience wears thin, Gary steps in. By some improbable coincidence, he was holding the very book Suzy needed to return. Grateful and intrigued by this strange twist of fate, Suzy offers to buy Gary a coffee.*

Their little coffee date got extended a bit too long. Their conversation, fueled by a shared love of books, quickly evolved into a marathon discussion about life, love, and everything in between. Enjoying each other's company, they ended up at a local bar for drinks after having coffee.

Hours later, tipsy and overwhelmed by the night's spontaneity, they pass a church renowned for its quirky, spur-of-the-moment weddings. In a hazy blur, they find themselves inside, standing before a priest who also happened to be a former rock star. Under the flickering neon lights of the chapel, they exchange vows, hardly grasping the reality of what they'd just done.

The next morning, as the weight of their impulsive decision begins to settle in, Suzy's relatives arrive one by one, each bringing their own brand of absurdity to an already bizarre situation. What fate awaits Suzy and Gary's marriage? Will their spontaneous decision lead to a lifetime of unexpected joy, or will the pressures from family and the reality of their hasty union pull them apart?

Aunt May:

Aunt May, the family's self-acclaimed-relationship-expert-gossip-queen, waltzed into Suzy's cramped living room, pausing dramatically with hands on her hips and pouting her lips at Suzy. She was clearly in dismay, her flamboyant entrance at odds with the gloomy mood inside.

May had expected to walk into a scene of wedded bliss, but was startled to find the couple locked in a heated debate over whether to order Chinese or pizza. The apartment, cluttered with stacks of books and mismatched furniture, felt more like a chaotic literary den than a newlyweds' love nest.

"My Suzy darling, I'm so thrilled for you! Hope I'm not interrupting anything... spicy," she chirped, her voice laced with innuendo as she pulled Suzy into a tight embrace.

May reached over to pull Gary into the same hug, unbothered by his evident discomfort and stiff posture.

"I had to see it with my own eyes! The whole family is buzzing about this." She said, playfully tapping Gary's chin, making him wince slightly.

Mortified, Suzy responded with a strained smile, trying to mask her unease.

Aunt May dumped her delicate, beaded purse and sat in the centre of the three-seater sofa, insisting they both sit on either side of her.

Wrapping one hand around Suzy's arms, she said, "Quite the looker, isn't he?"

Suzy thought the only thing more embarrassing than this moment would be if someone had broadcast the previous night's blunder live on television for all her friends and family to see.

Desperate to change the subject, Suzy interjected, "We were just about to order food, Aunt May. What would you like?"

She knew Aunt was a foodie, and thankfully, her little tactic worked. May's eyes lit up at the mention of food.

"Oh, darling, you must order dessert, too! We simply have to celebrate. And where's that bottle of wine I brought you last time?"

"Uh, yes, I still have it," Suzy muttered. *So, her Aunt would be staying longer than she'd anticipated.* Suzy wept inwardly.

"Don't worry, I'll get it." Gary glanced at her and sprinted to the kitchen before she could answer.

"Oh! A gentleman, too. You've come a long way, my darling", her Aunt mused like a soft romantic, cupping Suzy's flushed cheeks.

Suzy forced a smile, the absurdity of the situation sinking in deeper with every word her Aunt uttered.

May was the youngest of all her aunts. She was a psychotherapist by profession and a hopeless romantic by compulsion—a combination she claimed qualified her to prime all her blossoming nieces into adulthood. Suzy had some not-so-fond memories of her Aunt setting her up on blind dates during her early days in the city and of the countless free sessions where she was terrorised by the 'analysis of her patterns' with men. Her Aunt was ecstatic when she found out her lovely niece had moved nearby.

Ironically, she had never married nor been in love herself but enjoyed endlessly quizzing and advising family members, especially the younger ones, about their love lives.

"I know the news would have spread and rattled the entire family by now, but thank you for being supportive and turning up today," Suzy said in a low, sombre tone. Gary and I spoke earlier today and decided it's better to get it annulled."

Her Aunt stared with her mouth wide open.

Suzy added quickly, "-But nothing is final yet. Also, we would like to keep it low-key until then."

"No!" her Aunt cried out so loud that Gary had to bend backwards from the topmost shelf while searching for the wine glasses to see what was happening. "But you seem perfect for each other. Why not give it a shot? I have a good hunch about this"

Suzy bit her tongue, merely nodding. "Yes, we will think it over. Now, where was I.." She reached for her phone to resume the food order. It was almost two in the afternoon.

"So pizza it is, then?" Gary returned with the wine, sitting at least four feet apart from her Aunt this time. He turned on some music, dimmed the lights, and poured each of them a glass.

"Wow, you have great taste in music. I love jazz too", cooed Aunt May.

Oblivious to the tension, Aunt May's chatter turned back to her favourite subject—love. "You two are perfect together! Why rush into annulment talk? You know, I always knew you'd find someone special, Suzy. It's all about timing and taking a chance, even if it's a bit unexpected, like this!"

Suzy sighed in resignation. The sun was at its peak now. Suzy felt proud of herself for making it through half the day. She sat on the couch, relaxing with her legs folded and resting her head on May's shoulder. Her anxious thoughts began to ebb as they were replaced by the soft murmur of voices talking about music, art, and food.

A slight smile touched her face when she heard her Aunt ask Gary, "So, tell me more about yourself".

Cousin Daisy:

Daisy stepped into the apartment with a broad smile, her eyes scanning the room with thinly veiled judgment.

Noting the shabby furniture, a haphazard pile of books and the torn arm of the three-seater sofa she was seated in, Daisy said, "It's such a cute, cosy little apartment,"

Her smile betrayed the emptiness of her words as her gloss-tinted lips formed a forced curve on a face generously coated with makeup, glancing over at Suzy in the kitchen.

Suzy rolled her eyes before pouring tea into three differently-sized cups. She must be having a ball with this, she thought, knowing full well what Daisy must be thinking.

Gary, trying to break the tension, offered, "We were just talking about replacing the sofa."

Again, Daisy's smile didn't reach her eyes. "But I think it has character...Just like the two of you, I suppose," she replied, her words stinging Suzy like a bee.

Suzy and Daisy were cousins of the same age. Growing up together, they were pretty close. Their early years were full of summer vacations spent under each other's roofs, dressing the same, riding for hours on their bikes accompanied by endless chatter and giggles. They went for tennis and dance classes together, drawing sketches of their future rental apartment after landing their first jobs in the city.

Unfortunately, by high school, Suzy was sent off to boarding school while Daisy's parents were too scared to broach the topic because her adolescent tantrums were getting worse than her acne scars. Despite their bond, there was always an undercurrent of rivalry between them. Suzy was older by a few months. Bright, intellectual, and effortlessly beautiful, she often found herself unwittingly in the spotlight, which only fueled Daisy's attention-seeking, snotty demeanour.

Although they never had a chance to rent an apartment together, they stayed close over the years, sweet exchanges, tight hugs, and caring words softening the unmistakable tension whenever they met or spoke—just like this moment when Suzy was compelled by life's circumstances to face her cousin in her messy albeit 'cosy' one-bedroom apartment with a less-than-a-day-old husband.

"So, Mom and Aunt Annie will be arriving tomorrow. They can stay at my place, you know. I am sure they would like to give you some privacy", Daisy smirked, taking the cup from Suzy.

As if her head wasn't throbbing from the hangover already, the thought of how Daisy would recount this union to the rest of the family induced a sense of panic.

She had the urge to dial her mother's number immediately but responded instead, "It's fine, I have made arrangements for their stay. We will shift to his apartment."

Gary nodded and stood up, smiling earnestly at Daisy, "I will leave you two sisters to chat. It was lovely meeting you, Daisy. Please do visit us again", and left the room.

"He's cute! I don't blame you!" Daisy smacked her sister's arm, turning towards her with a mischievous grin.

Suzy shrugged, her headache worsening. "Yeah... it just happened. And I guess, now, we have to deal with it." Her hand caressed her forehead lightly.

"It's not that bad, from what I see. You seem compatible and obviously have common interests. Marriage could be fun."

Suzy wondered how Daisy could have made such sweeping judgments after spending less than thirty minutes with them. But that was her cousin Daisy—always quick to draw conclusions.

"How's Wells?" Suzy asked, trying to deflect the conversation away from her own predicament.

Daisy beamed, "Oh, he's great! He actually wants to take me on a vacation next month. He might want to move in for good after that, you know what I mean.." She paused to look at Suzy, her eyes twinkling after recognising she had understood very well what that meant.

"I mentioned your thing to him, and he is absolutely thrilled. We should all go out for dinner sometime. Gary would really like him, too.." She went on, her voice dripping with excitement.

Suzy nodded, half-smiling, half-listening as Daisy droned on about her perfect relationship. She took long sips from her cup, the warm tea slowly soothing and lifting her hangover, allowing the weight of last night's decisions to fall upon her.

Uncle Tim:

Uncle Tim drove through the neighbourhood with a furrowed brow, glancing at his wife, Ellie, who was peering curiously out the window. "Should we have brought a gift?" he asked, his voice tinged with uncertainty.

"It's too late for that now," Ellie responded distractedly. "Isn't there parking inside the building?"

"It's okay, we won't be long," Timothy reassured her, though he wasn't entirely sure himself.

It took some effort on Timothy Millis' part to convince his wife the neighbourhood was safe until she finally agreed to get out of the car. She had been sullen since the morning after Tim informed her that brunch with her girlfriends would have to be cancelled to attend to a most unique and urgent family matter.

Timothy's younger sister (Suzy's mother) had called him early in the morning, on the verge of hysteria, pleading him to meet with Suzy as soon as possible because her flight wouldn't leave until midnight. She said she trusted his opinion more than anyone else's in the family. Timothy obliged at once who, with his warm, amicable nature, was not just Suzy's uncle but a father figure to her. Suzy's father had passed away at an early age.

In fact, one of the reasons Suzy's mother did not mind her move to the new city was that Uncle Tim lived less than an hour's drive away. Besides, Suzy herself was extremely fond of him, always counting on his wisdom, tempered with laughter and kindness, to deal with life's crossroads.

However, stepping out of the car now, he wasn't so certain he knew the best way to deal with the current situation. It was more akin to an entangled mess. Regardless, his protectiveness towards Suzy meant he wouldn't have been at peace without making the drive down himself.

His thoughts were racing as he rang the doorbell, patting his wife's shoulder reassuringly. Suzy gasped as soon as she opened the door and saw her uncle holding a bouquet of flowers. Like a child who had found a parent after being lost in a bustling crowd, she hugged him as though he was the only person in the world she could bear to see at that moment.

"I'm sorry for the trouble. I know Mom must have called you. I know I have disappointed you," she said through muffled sobs, her tears spilling onto his shoulder.

"There, there, my child. You haven't disappointed anyone."

She felt Ellie's soft, manicured hands on her back, "We are excited to meet him. I was just telling your uncle on the way here."

"Now let's go in," he said, wrapping his arms around her in a comforting embrace, wiping off her tears, and walking in. Suzy leaned on his shoulder as if she had found the only adequate support for her turmoil of the past several hours, his steady presence reminding her she wasn't alone. Gary met them in the small hallway, having heard their teary union from a few meters behind.

The two men stood facing each other, their eyes locking in a silent acknowledgement of the new family dynamic. Gary greeted them politely and took their coats, his movements smooth and respectful as he led them to the sofa, which appeared squeaky clean. Suzy watched, her heart swelling with a mix of nervousness and a tinge of pride.

"Would you like some tea or coffee?" Suzy's voice cut through the palpable tension in the air.

"Tea is fine", Ellie responded.

"I had to make sure I visited you two before you jet off on your honeymoon or something", Uncle Tim said with his casual, half-joking flair, "Can't have you escaping before I had the chance to properly interrogate the new son-in-law, can I?"

Gary chuckled. "Glad you made it."

"So, what do you do for a living?"

"I'm an art director. I work at the Horizon on 458 Marlowe", Gary replied.

Uncle Tim's brows lifted approvingly, "Ah, that sounds fascinating. Must be quite challenging to bring artistic visions to life."

"Absolutely, it has its moments of frustration, but I find it incredibly rewarding. I've always believed that art has the power to tell stories in unique ways."

Noticing that Ellie felt left out of the conversation, Gary turned toward her and asked, "So, where are you folks from?"

She looked up from her phone, pleased to receive attention after feeling overlooked by the two men.

Suzy brought in the piping hot tea served on a tray with cookies and cake she'd ordered after anticipating her uncle's visit. As the afternoon progressed, the initial awkwardness that had hung in the air was replaced by laughter and discussions revolving around art, actors, celebs and movie-making, punctuated by her uncle's quick anecdotes.

Their exchanges seemed to be brimming with genuine interest and mutual respect, and Suzy felt a warm glow of relief, much warmer than Ellie's smile.

By the time they were ready to leave, two hours had passed, and everyone felt too tired and too comfortable to get up. Shaking hands with Gary, Uncle Tim beckoned him to visit him sometime and kissed his niece's cheek before stepping through the door onto the curbside, where his car was neatly parked. He gracefully slid into the driver's seat while Ellie slipped in next to him and said, "Until next time." Waving at them, Gary circled his arms around Suzy, watching them go.

Later that evening, when Gary was washing the dishes in the kitchen, Suzy could not stop smiling as she read and reread her uncle's text message over and over. '*I like him*' – he had written.

The Digital Minimalist

"The greatest wealth is to live content with little."

- Plato

Anuj was drowning—not in water but in a sea of notifications, emails, and endless tabs. His small apartment, cluttered with piles of unopened boxes, empty coffee cups, and a tangle of charging cables, mirrored the chaos in his mind. He'd been staring at his computer screen for hours, the initial thrill of a free Saturday morning replaced by a growing sense of dread as he toggled between work emails and his savings app.

His goal was simple: save enough for a down payment on a cosy apartment in the city. But every time he opened his finance app, a shiny new gadget or a tempting travel deal would distract him. The temptation to indulge was always there, fueled by his fast-paced life, which Sai, his best friend since college, seemed to handle with ease.

Sai was the epitome of success. A tech entrepreneur with a knack for spotting the latest trends, he thrived in a world of constant stimulation. His boundless energy and enthusiasm were infectious, making him the life of every party and the go-to person for career and tech advice. Anuj admired Sai's drive but secretly resented the pressure to keep up with his lifestyle. His world felt like a rollercoaster he couldn't keep up with, and though he tried to mirror it, the effort only left him feeling more drained.

"You're turning into a real hermit", Sai teased over the phone. "When was the last time you actually left your apartment?"

"Just trying to stay focused," Anuj mumbled into his pillow. "Saving up for that apartment, remember?"

Sai laughed. "Save money? Invest in yourself, man. Look at me. I work hard, but I also know how to enjoy life. You need to get out there, network, and expand your horizons."

Anuj sighed, feeling a pang of frustration. He knew Sai meant well, but his lifestyle felt unattainable. Could he really balance saving money and living more freely? His mind drifted back to his cluttered apartment and the never-ending to-do lists. Maybe Sai had a point. He was taking the 'save money' mantra too far. He needed a change, something drastic.

The following day, Anuj sat at the kitchen table, scrolling through his endless feed. His eyes glazed over until a headline caught his attention: "Digital Minimalism: Live a Focused & Fulfilling Life." Intrigued, he clicked the article. As he read, the cluttered room around him seemed to fade away. This was it. This was the reset button he needed.
The article discussed the importance of intentional living, focusing on what truly matters, and simplifying one's life. It was as if the writer had peered into Anuj's soul and spelled out his problems. Anuj decided to give it a shot. He would eliminate distractions, focus on his finances, and maybe, just maybe, find a better balance in life.

Over the next few days, Anuj's apartment, once a battlefield of scattered papers, empty food wrappers, and electronic debris, began to transform. Inspired, he started small, throwing away a few boxes here, organising a drawer there. With ruthless efficiency, he cleared his desk, a monstrous behemoth covered in a labyrinth of wires, sticky notes, and half-finished projects, leaving only a laptop, a notepad, and a pen. The rest found their way into boxes, destined for the trash.

He deleted unused apps, silenced notifications, and turned off unnecessary features. With each step, from clearing the clutter to organising his digital files, Anuj felt a growing sense of liberation. The transformation was gradual but impactful.

As days turned into weeks, Anuj found himself spending more time outdoors, engaging in activities he'd long neglected. Mindless scrolling was replaced by walks in the park, and quick meal deliveries gave way to the simple pleasure of cooking his own meals.

He rediscovered the joy of reading physical books, the satisfaction of a handwritten letter, and the warmth of human connection. Slowly, he rekindled his social life as well, as he started attending game nights on Fridays, where he befriended two other guys with whom camaraderie came easy. They began meeting for a game of tennis at least twice a week. Gradually, the fog in his mind started to clear, replaced by a sense of purpose. Anuj could feel the transformation as his body grew more robust and productivity skyrocketed. He was in and felt his best shape.

Sitting at a café with his friend Deepak one evening, Anuj shared about his newfound lifestyle. "I've never felt this free," Anuj said, smiling. "It's like I've finally found the time to live."

Deepak raised an eyebrow. "It's great to hear, man. But how's work handling this change?"

Anuj shrugged, a smile creeping onto his face. "Honestly, never been better. I've been able to focus better, and my boss noticed. Last week, I walked into the office, and he called me in. Thought I was in trouble at first," Anuj chuckled, "but he offered me a promotion. Said he was impressed with my work lately."

Deepak's eyes widened in admiration. "Congratulations! This has really paid off for you."

Anuj nodded, taking a sip of his detox drink.

But life, as it often does, had other plans. His well-earned job promotion started demanding more of his time until the pressure became overwhelming. Urgent emails, unexpected video calls, and mandatory online meetings began to creep back into his life. The carefully constructed digital walls he'd erected started to crumble. Some days, it felt as if he had gone hundreds of steps back, finding himself caught in a tug-of-war between his desire for digital freedom and the demands of his professional life.

One day, during their weekly coffee catch-up at the office, his colleague Priya commented, "You're looking a bit frazzled lately.", noticing the dark circles under his eyes. "What happened to the whole minimalist thing?"

Anuj sighed deeply, rubbing his temples. "It's like trying to swim upstream," he replied, the frustration evident in his voice. "I'm drowning in notifications and deadlines again."

Priya nodded sympathetically. "Maybe it's time to find a balance," she suggested. "You don't have to be completely off the grid to benefit from minimalism, you know?"

As he finished his coffee, Anuj pondered her words. She was right. *Had he been too rigid in his approach?* Maybe minimalism wasn't about complete isolation but about intentional living. With renewed determination, Anuj walked back to his desk and decided to experiment. He set boundaries for his digital consumption – specific hours for emails, social media, and online meetings. The rest of the time would be dedicated to offline activities and personal growth.

It wasn't easy. There were days when the digital world beckoned irresistibly. But Anuj persisted, reminding himself of the peace he had found in his simpler routine. Slowly, steadily, a new equilibrium began to emerge. He was connected but not consumed. As weeks turned into months, these new habits solidified. Once again, his work became productive, relationships deepened, and mental clarity blossomed.

One weekend, as he sat in his living room, surrounded by a few carefully chosen objects, he felt a sense of contentment he hadn't experienced in a long time. The digital noise had subsided, replaced by the gentle ticking of the clock. His past life of clutter and distractions seemed like a distant memory. Life was no longer a race against endless deadlines.
He relaxed on the chair, quietly enjoying the sunset from his windows. Just as he was about to settle into a book, his phone buzzed.
It was Sai.

"Hey, man," Anuj answered, a smile in his voice.

"Anuj! Long time no see. How's the hermit life treating you?" Sai teased, his voice crackling with energy.

Anuj chuckled. "I've found a nice balance. How about you?"

"Balance, huh? Well, you know me. Work's been crazy, but I love it. I'm grinding non-stop, barely getting any sleep, but that's how you get ahead, right? It's all about the hustle!" Sai's voice brimmed with pride.

Anuj listened, the old anxiety trying to creep in but unable to take hold this time. He replied calmly, "That's amazing. More power to you."

There was a brief pause on the line before Sai spoke again, his tone slightly incredulous. "But seriously? You're not worried about falling behind? I mean, come on, man, you were always the one trying to keep up."

Anuj shook his head, feeling more confident than ever. "I'm not worried, Sai."

Sai laughed, a bit more forcefully this time. "So you're a content man now? Wow, that's not in my vocabulary! But hey, if you're happy, that's what matters, I guess."

"It is what matters," Anuj nodded gently.

After they hung up, Anuj put down his phone and leaned back in his chair, stretching lazily and basking in the quiet satisfaction of knowing he'd finally saved enough for his down payment. The sun dipped below the horizon, casting a warm glow over the room as he realised he had found something far greater than a well-organised space or a streamlined schedule—he had found a home within himself.

Barnaby Bunkle's Dilemma

The Magic in Second Chances

Nestled beneath the towering Mooseburry Mountains, the quaint village of Yoreville was a hidden world of wonders. Here, a community of hardy folk steeped in ancient knowledge thrived with their hands in the rich earth, cultivating an array of enchanted crops and mystical plants. Some of these crops were infused with magic—glowing moonflowers that bloomed under the stars, golden wheat that whispered secrets in the wind, and berries with the power to heal the deepest wounds.

Life was simple and peaceful in Yoreville. The villagers went about their daily tasks with quiet contentment, though some, like Barnaby Bunkle, carried a heavier burden.

Generations of farmers and tradesmen called this place home. It was a vibrant crossroads where enchanted harvests mingled with exotic treasures brought by wandering merchants. Each week, the villagers eagerly awaited the arrival of these merchants, ready to barter for fresh farm produce, spices, intricate handicrafts, and the occasional alluring trinket, each promising a hint of the unknown.

One balmy autumn afternoon, the most enigmatic of these tradesmen, who went by the name Reginald the Remarkable, rolled into town with a gleaming smile. His wagon, creaking under the weight of shimmering trinkets, mysterious vials, and otherworldly artefacts, wore signs that promised *'Worlds Beyond Imagination'*. Glowing orbs floated above it, casting eerie shadows, and a trail of sweet-smelling smoke followed him as he made his way into the village, holding something miraculous. His self-assured swagger and the fervour with which he announced his arrival suggested a man utterly convinced of his own importance. Yet, the villagers crowded around him every time he visited, eager to see his extravagant displays. Some came simply to watch as if attending a grand spectacle, waiting to witness the villagers exchange their prized possessions for Reginald's innovative items.

As he held up his latest wonder, all eyes were fixed on him.

"Behold, the ChronoCarpet!" Reginald declared, his voice echoing through the village square. With one swift movement, he unfolded a luxurious red carpet woven with threads that seemed to dance in the sunlight.

"This magical carpet can transport you to any timeline in your life!"

The villagers were transfixed. He continued, "Yes, you heard that right. You can go back to any time. Relive your greatest moments, rectify your biggest mistakes and failures, anything you like". A hush fell over the crowd as they stared in disbelief, imagining the possibilities. Old Mrs. Willow, known for her sharp wit, squinted at the carpet and asked boldly, "And how, pray tell, does one return?"

Reginald, undeterred by her scepticism, flashed a confident grin. "Fear not, good people," he replied, his voice dripping with assurance. The

ChronoCarpet is a two-way ticket. You'll return to this very spot, at this very moment, but a wealth of experiences richer." He paused, his expression turning somewhat sombre, then added, "But remember, there are rules: you may revisit up to three events but can change only one."

Gasps and murmurs of awe rippled through the crowd. The hefty price tag he quoted left the villagers exchanging incredulous glances. Their minds raced with the implications of this device as they imagined both the benefits and risks of such a bargain.

Barnaby Bunkle, a perpetually grumpy and resentful 40-year-old farmer, was most intrigued. He had spent years brooding over his misfortune, unable to come to terms with his past. Determined to seize this opportunity, Barnaby sold his prized oxen, his grandmother's heirloom silverware, and even his beloved collection of rare potato varieties to afford the coveted ChronoCarpet.

Clutching his newly acquired treasure as if it were his last hope, Barnaby retreated to his humble cottage, feeling the weight of his choices. With trembling hands, he unfurled the ChronoCarpet in his living room. It now appeared worn and threadbare, a stark contrast to the staggering expense he had to bear. A sense of dread mingled with his hope. Could this really change his life? Or was it just another cruel trick, like the ones life had already played on him?

Taking a deep breath and a muttered prayer, he stepped onto the intricate weave, heart pounding in his chest. The room spun around him in a dizzying vortex, and in a flash of light, he was transported to his first chosen moment - it was the day he lost the love of his life, Marcella.

Barnaby found himself hovering above the scene where she was about to depart the village for the city, leaving him heartbroken. Dapper and earnest, his younger self stood arguing with Marcella by the well. She was vibrant and full of dreams, her eyes sparkling with the excitement of a future in the city.
"Come with me, Barnaby," she pleaded. "We could start a new life together. There's a whole world out there beyond these fields."
"I can't leave the farm, Marcella", young Barnaby insisted, his voice filled with reluctance. "It's my family's legacy."
"But your heart yearns for more than this, Barnaby. And you *know* it," Eliza countered gently. "Your knowledge of herbs is a gift. Here, it's so limited. Imagine the possibilities in the city. With access to rare ingredients and mentors, you can create remedies that could help countless people."
Barnaby was silent, his mind racing. Herbalism had always been his passion. The idea of dedicating his life to it was appealing, but the thought of leaving his younger brother to manage the farm all by himself weighed heavily on his conscience. After their parents passed away, he'd been a father figure,

a protector, and a provider to him. How could he abandon him now?

Watching from above, Barnaby felt a pang of regret. He saw the anguish in Marcella's eyes as she told him she loved him but couldn't pass up the opportunity to move to the city. He wanted to shout down, to tell his younger self to go with her, to warn himself of the opportunities slipping away. As Barnaby watched Marcella walk away, his heart ached with a longing he had buried for years. The memory of her fading silhouette was etched in his mind, yet now, from this vantage point, he saw not just the pain of loss but the opportunities he had let slip by. He wanted to shout down, to tell his younger self to go with her and live his dreams. He lingered, reluctant to move on, as if hoping she might turn back and offer him one last chance… But he knew he couldn't change this moment without considering the next. So, with a heavy heart, he watched Marcella leave.

After a few moments, he decided to move to the next pivotal scene of his life. The scene shifted, transporting Barnaby to the bustling village marketplace roughly three years after Marcella left him. There, he saw a younger, eager version of himself being approached by a slick, silver-tongued tradesman peddling magical seeds that promised a bountiful harvest.

"These seeds will bring you fortune beyond your wildest dreams," the tradesman declared with a

persuasive grin. "A crop so abundant, you'll never worry about money again."
As Barnaby watched, a knot of anticipation formed in his stomach. He knew this moment was pivotal. His younger self, eyes sparkling with hope and greed, was on the brink of making a fateful decision. The younger Barnaby reached for his purse, ready to hand over his hard-earned savings.

Just as his fingers brushed against the coins, a tiny detail caught Barnaby's attention.
The tradesman wore a small, intricate amulet that flickered whenever he spoke of the seeds' magic. A surge of recognition coursed through Barnaby. His father had once shown him the power of such an amulet, a rare device capable of detecting lies. It was a secret not known to many. The dimming of its light was a subtle yet clear sign of the tradesman's deceit. Exhilaration washed over Barnaby. If he had been more perceptive in the past, he could have exposed the scam, demanded the genuine magical seeds, and secured a life of prosperity. The possibilities were intoxicating. He felt he had unlocked a precious key and realized this was the mistake he had to rectify. He would acquire the genuine seeds, cultivate a bountiful harvest, and share the wealth with his brother. Then, he would reunite with Marcella in the city and pursue his passions.

Just as he imagined his happily-ever-after, a shadow of doubt crept into his mind. The third and final event loomed large—the bitter argument with his brother, Amos, that had severed their relationship forever. Could he truly repair the damage, or would his interference create unforeseen consequences?

Just then, the scene shifted, and Barnaby found himself in his old kitchen, watching a heated argument unfold between himself and Amos. The air was thick with tension as they shouted over each other.

"You never support my ideas!" Amos yelled. "You always think you're so much smarter than me."

"It's not about being smarter, Amos," Barnaby retorted. "It's about being sensible. Those magical seeds were a scam, and you were too blind to see it!"

"Blind? You were the one who fell for it!" Amos shot back. "You lost everything, and now you're dragging me down with you."

"So what? We will build it back!"

"I don't want to build anything back with you. You can never manage things the way Father did."

Barnaby watched in horror as the argument escalated, culminating in Amos storming out, vowing never to return. He realized that his own failures had fueled the fight, his pride and stubbornness driving a wedge between them.

Hovering above and seeing the interconnectedness of these events, his thoughts raced once again. If he had secured the genuine magical seeds, he would have become wealthy, and the argument with Amos might never have happened. But this realization brought him to a grave dilemma: Was it worthwhile going back and fixing the scam, becoming wealthy, and possibly mending his relationship with Amos, or should he revisit the moment with Marcella to regain her love, move to the city and follow his passions?

The desire for wealth and longing for lost love tugged at him in equal measure.

Barnaby's mind wrestled with conflicting emotions. If he fixed the scam, wealth would be within his grasp, and perhaps he could mend things with Amos. But at what cost? Could he live with the knowledge that his newfound fortune was built on altering the past? Would it truly heal the rift with Amos? And what of Marcella? Was it fair to rekindle their relationship based on a life that never truly was?

The weight of these questions pressed down upon him, filling him with uncertainty. He realized that altering one event might not provide the perfect solution he longed for but, in turn, create new complications he could not foresee. The temptation to rewrite his past had been undeniably strong when he set out on his magic carpet, but now, after watching the scenes play out before him like a tragic play, his perspective had shifted entirely. Barnaby stood at a crossroads, his heart and mind in turmoil, pondering whether it was better to embrace his imperfect life or risk unravelling it entirely.

With a deep sigh, Barnaby made his decision and stepped off the ChronoCarpet. The magic dissipated, and he was back in his humble cottage, surrounded by the familiarity of his unaltered life. But now, everything looked different. He was poorer in coin, perhaps, but richer in understanding. His regrets no longer haunted him.

He felt a deep sense of gratitude as he realized that his life, with all its imperfections, was his own unique story, and for the first time in years, a genuine smile tugged at the corners of his mouth.

The next day, the villagers noticed a transformation in Barnaby. His usual grumpy demeanour had softened, replaced by a cheerful and thoughtful presence. Curious, they asked him what he had altered in the past. He simply smiled and responded with the same words every time, *"Absolutely Nothing"*.

As for Reginald the Remarkable, he departed Yoreville a much wealthier man, his wagon laden with new riches. With a knowing glint in his eye, he cast one final glance at the village. He had always known what the outcome of sitting on that magic carpet would be.

The truth was that it offered more than just a chance to change the past; it offered the opportunity to change themselves. And that was the *real* magic of the ChronoCarpet.

11:11

To new beginnings

The bathroom mirror was completely fogged from the steam as Hemalatha stepped out of the shower, droplets of water tracing paths down the glass. Her thick, long hair hung in damp, unruly waves, clinging stubbornly to her back as a reminder of the warmth she had just left behind.

Wrapping herself in a towel, her feet padded softly across the wooden floor to the small corner of her room where she had set up a makeshift shrine. A tiny idol of Lord Ganesha, intricately carved and brought from Bangalore, India, sat atop a small shelf. The shrine was a simple affair—just a brass lamp, some incense sticks, and occasionally a few fresh flowers. But to her, it was a piece of home that she carried with her across continents. Hema lit the incense and closed her eyes, clasping her hands together.

The delicate tendrils of incense smoke mingled with the low murmur of the city, creating a peaceful ambience for her prayer. Within the confines of her small studio apartment, the ticking of the wall clock echoed softly as its hands aligned at 11:11 am. She felt a gentle wave of possibility wash over her for a moment.

It was almost time to leave for her class. She turned to her tiny wardrobe, a modest piece of furniture that barely accommodated her limited collection of clothes. Her fingers brushed past the few hanging garments before settling on a plain, blue tunic—a familiar choice that brought her a sense of comfort in this foreign land.

As Hema began to dress, the sound of her phone ringing pulled her from her thoughts. Reaching for it, her heart warmed at the sight of Meera's picture on the screen. *What a beautiful young woman she has become,* she mused, a smile softening her features as the corners of her eyes crinkled with the well-earned lines of age. Despite the distance between them, this daily connection with her daughter was a lifeline on this new journey.

"*Amma*? Good morning!" Meera's voice was brighter than the weather outside.
"Good morning, Meera! How are you, *kanna*?" Hemalatha asked, her heart lifting at the sound of her daughter's voice.
"I'm good, *Amma*. Just finished an assignment. How's Paris treating you today?"
"Paris is... busy, as always", Hemalatha replied, glancing out the window at the narrow street below. "But I'm getting used to it. The school is very hectic, but I'm learning so much."
"I'm sure you are. It must be amazing to finally be pursuing your passion."
"It is", she replied, thinking of the delicate éclairs and flaky puff pastries she had been practising. "It's hard work, but it's worth it. I feel... alive again."
There was a long pause on the other end of the line before Meera spoke again, her tone more serious. "*Amma,* are you sure you're ready for all of this? It's

such a big change, and I worry about you being so far away."

Hemalatha teared up slightly, touched by her daughter's concern. "I understand, Meera. But I needed this. After everything that happened… I needed to find myself again. And yes, this.. this new life, it's what I want. I'm ready for it."

Meera sighed, but it was a sound of acceptance. "Okay, as long as you're happy, that's all that matters. I just want you to take care of yourself, okay?"

"I will, *kanna*. Don't worry about me. I'm doing what I love, and that's enough."

They exchanged a few more words before hanging up. Hema placed the phone down with a deep exhale. Meera was right. This city was a world away from what she was used to, but it was here that she had chosen to rebuild herself. The thought brought a renewed sense of purpose as she dressed, preparing to step out for the day.

The walk to the culinary academy was one she had come to enjoy. The cobblestone streets were uneven but made her steps deliberate, even mindful, as if each footfall was there to ground herself. On either side, vibrant bouquets of fresh flowers spilled onto the sidewalk, their petals kissed by the morning sun. Hema had memorized the path by now. She would often stop outside the boulangerie to admire the intricate window displays of artisanal chocolates, the dark and glossy truffles arranged with an artistry that spoke of the French reverence for food. The city was waking up, and with each step, she felt herself waking up, too.

The academy's grand facade soon came into view, standing tall with its weathered stone. It was a historic building known throughout France for producing some of the finest chefs in the world. Hemalatha had been both thrilled and terrified when she first walked through its doors, but over time, she had come to see it as a place where she could rekindle the passion for cooking that had always burned within her.

As she entered the bustling hallways of the school, the smell of butter and sugar enveloped her, reminding her of how exhilarating it was to be here. This was her chance to start anew, to take all the love and care she had poured into her family and direct it toward something that was just for her. Today, she would be working on perfecting her *mille-feuille,* a pastry as complex as it was beautiful—a fitting symbol for her own metamorphosis. Hemalatha straightened her shoulders and walked into the kitchen.

As she made her way to her workstation, the hall was already alive with activity. "*Buongiorno,* Hema!" called out Gerald, his Italian accent thick and musical. He was already at his station, a blur of motion prepping his ingredients.

"Good morning, Gerald", Hema greeted him with a bright smile.

Gerald's face always lit up when Hema spoke his name. It was an impulsive response to the motherly affection in her tone. Being in his early twenties, he had a vitality that often left his older classmates struggling to keep up. When he first met Hema, he was immediately drawn to her calm and nurturing spirit. Their connection quickly deepened into a special bond. Having been an orphan and raised in a series of foster homes, Gerald had never experienced the steady presence of a parental figure, and in a short time, Hema had become that figure for him—a source of wisdom, advice and the occasional reprimand when his enthusiasm got the better of him.

"You're ready to conquer the *mille-feuille* today, yes?" Gerald asked, his eyes sparkling with excitement.

"I'm ready to try", Hema laughed, her spirit buoyed by his youthfulness.

Their laughter drew the attention of Christine, who approached with her usual confident gait, the click-clack of her heels announcing her arrival. Tall, with a sharp bob of chestnut hair and a pair of glasses perched on her nose, Christine had an air of effortless sophistication. Prior to joining the academy, she was an editor at one of Britain's most prestigious fashion magazines. It was a position that had demanded every ounce of her time and energy until, one day, she decided to quit.

"Morning, Hem", Christine greeted, her tone polite but warmer than it had been in the early days of their acquaintance.

"Good morning, Christine", Hema replied, appreciating the gradual thawing in Christine's demeanour.

When they first met, Christine was cold and distant, and her polished exterior was difficult to penetrate. Hema's kindness and persistence had slowly chipped away at Christine's walls, revealing the woman beneath—the one who was exhausted from years of relentless deadlines and high-stakes decisions and was now embracing a slower pace and indulging her love for cooking.
It was over kitchen mishaps and long conversations after classes that the three of them, from different walks of life, had forged an unlikely friendship that transformed the arduous days at the academy into something genuinely fulfilling.

As the day's lesson progressed, Hema was immersed in her task, her hands moving with practised ease as she layered the buttery pastry. Just as she was about to complete her 'dessert of the day,' her knife slipped, sending a sharp pain lancing through her finger. The sudden sting and the sight of blood brought a rush of memories—Hema was no longer in the academy but back in her kitchen in Bangalore, the sweet aroma of baking filling the air as she prepared a cake for her children. She had cut her finger then, too, and Sanjeev, her husband at the time, had rushed to her side. He had taken her hand in his, concern etched on his face, and gently bandaged her finger. It was one of those rare moments when they had felt close, a time before everything had gone wrong.

Hema blinked, pushing the memory aside as she quickly wrapped a bandage around her finger. But the past lingered in her mind, and she couldn't help but think back to her life before Paris.
Back then, Hemalatha's days were a symphony of routine—waking up early, preparing meals, attending to her children's needs, and supporting her husband, Sanjeev, whose career always took precedence before anything. As a devoted wife and mother of two, her world revolved entirely around her family, while her aspirations faded into the background. The dreams she once had of becoming a chef were quietly shelved soon after marriage, buried beneath the weight of household responsibilities and the relentless demands of motherhood.

For years, she found contentment in the rhythm of her daily life, all the while silently nurturing a love for cooking that never saw the light of day. But on the eve of her 43rd birthday, everything turned upside down, and her world crumbled. A misplaced mobile phone, a series of clandestine messages, and a confrontation that left her speechless unveiled a truth she had never imagined.
That evening, Hema sat at the dining table, her heart pounding as she waited for her husband to come home. When he finally walked through the door,

she could barely contain the emotions swirling inside her.

"Sanjeev", she called out, her voice trembling but resolute. "We need to talk."

He paused, sensing the tension in the air. "What is it, Hema?" he asked, his tone laced with impatience as he set his briefcase down.

Hema held up the phone, her hand shaking. "I found this in your jacket pocket today. There were messages, Sanjeev. Who is she?"

Sanjeev's face drained of colour, his usual confident demeanour faltering for just a moment before he quickly regained composure. "Hema, it's not what you think—"

"Not what I think?" Hema's voice rose, a mix of disbelief and anger fueling her words. "Then explain to me what it is! Is it true? For how long, Sanjeev?"

He hesitated, searching for words that might soften the blow, but there were none. "It's been... a while," he finally admitted, his eyes avoiding hers.

"A while? How long, Sanjeev? How long have you been lying to me?" Her voice cracked, the weight of betrayal pressing down on her.

A few tense seconds passed. Sanjeev finally broke the silence. "Over eleven years," he confessed quietly, his voice barely audible.

Hema felt like she had been struck by a truck, the revelation hitting her with the force of a slow-motion car crash—devastating yet inescapable. The words echoed in her mind, each syllable slicing through the very fabric of the life she had thought she knew.

"Eleven years?" she repeated, her voice trembling with disbelief. "Eleven years, Sanjeev?"

The ground seemed to slip from beneath her feet, weakening her legs. She collapsed to the floor, her fingers gripping the table's edge. In an instant, tears erupted from her face as she struggled to quell the storm of emotions raging within her. The room seemed to close in around her. Their former haven now lay in ruins. Hema felt as though she were consumed by its wreckage, her heart breaking under the unbearable weight of betrayal.

Seeing the depth of her despair, Sanjeev tried to reach out, but Hema recoiled at once, the pain too raw, too deep. "Don't touch me," she whispered, her voice thick with emotion. "Everything was a lie. *Everything*."

He did not say a word. His silence was a stark acknowledgement of the irreparable damage he had caused.

At first, she refused to believe it, clinging to the hope that it was a misunderstanding. But as the days passed, the reality of the betrayal seeped into her consciousness, leaving her in a state of numbness for months. When she finally confronted Sanjeev, hoping for an apology, a reconciliation, something to make sense of it all, he simply asked for a divorce. The words hit her like a sledgehammer, cold and detached. She felt her life shattering into a million pieces. All that she had carefully built, the sacrifices she had made, all gone in an instant.

For a year after the divorce, Hema drifted through life like a ghost, haunted by the memories of a life that no longer existed. The home that once echoed with laughter now felt like a cold, empty tomb of broken vows. Desperate to escape, she spent months living with friends and relatives, hoping that distance would numb the ache. Yet, wherever she turned, the remnants of her failed marriage and the societal stigma of being a divorced woman in a conservative society cast a long, dark shadow.

In a culture where a woman's worth was often tied to her role as a wife and mother, Hema found herself unceremoniously stripped of the only identities she had known for decades. The pitying glances, the hushed conversations behind her back, and the judgmental stares only deepened her sense of isolation. Her children, Meera and Ved, tried to offer their support, but they were just beginning to forge their own paths—Meera was just starting college and Ved, his first internship. Though they loved her dearly, they were young, with lives of their own to build.

It became painfully clear to Hema that she could no longer depend on the roles and relations that had once defined her. The realization dawned that she needed to build herself from scratch, to find a purpose that was wholly her own. On an impulse, she applied to a prestigious culinary school in France. The kitchen was always her solace, a constant in a world of change, and it was only natural she would turn to it in her time of need. She poured her heart into the application, not truly believing she would be accepted but feeling compelled to do something, anything, to break free from the confines of her former life. When the acceptance letter arrived, she was shocked. It felt like life had given her a second chance.

At 45, Hemalatha Rao made the bold decision to leave everything she had ever known behind and move to a new country. With nothing but a suitcase and an education loan, partially funded by her alimony, she set out to pick up the pieces of her life. The path ahead was fraught with uncertainty and challenges, but it was the only way forward. Her decision was met with surprise and concern from family and friends. But Hema was resolute, more certain than she had ever been.

With its rich culinary heritage, France was as unfamiliar as it was enticing. Each day felt like an emotional rollercoaster, be it grappling with the language barrier, navigating the unknown streets all by herself, struggling to decipher the menus written in elegant French script, or communicating with classmates half her age. There were days when she felt like giving up, packing her bags, and returning home. But every time she entered the kitchen, all her doubts melted away.

The culinary school was as demanding as it was prestigious. The long hours, the rigorous training, and the exacting standards pushed Hema to her limits. It wasn't just the cooking that was challenging. Hema had to adjust to the French way of life, the tiny apartments, the brisk manners, the endless bureaucracy. But in the midst of all this, she found solace in the chopping of vegetables, the sizzle of onions in a hot pan, and the aroma of freshly baked bread. Cooking became her language, her expression, and slowly, she began to find her footing.

The decision to join culinary school had, indeed, been nothing short of life-altering, a leap of faith that had brought her to this present moment in a busy kitchen surrounded by eager, aspiring chefs. Hema winced, the sting in her finger pulling her out of her thoughts. The physical discomfort was a sharp contrast to the mental ache that had briefly taken hold of her. Steadying her hands, she turned back to the task at hand. A *mille-feuille* demanded precision, patience, and unwavering attention—qualities she had honed through the years.

The following day in class, Hema was fully absorbed in the delicate task of poaching eggs, her hands gliding with the confidence that months of practice had instilled, when she suddenly sensed a presence behind her. A shadow fell across her workstation, and she looked up to see Chef Alain, the head instructor of the academy, standing there with an unreadable expression on his face.

"Hema, could I speak with you for a moment in my office?" he asked, his tone neutral but carrying an undercurrent of something she couldn't quite place.

Her heart skipped a beat, anxiety prickling at the edges of her mind. She nodded, setting down her tools and wiping her hands on her apron. As she followed Chef Alain through the kitchen and down the quiet hallways, her mind raced with the worst possibilities. *Had her fee payment been declined? Would they terminate her stay?*

Once they reached his office, Chef Alain closed the door behind them and motioned for her to sit. Hema complied, feeling a knot of tension forming in her stomach. He took a seat across from her, his usually stern face softened with a hint of a smile.

"Hema", he began, leaning forward slightly. "I've been watching your progress closely since you joined us, and I must say, your dedication and growth have not gone unnoticed. You have a natural talent, particularly with pastries."

Hema's breath caught in her throat so tight that she almost choked. She had worked hard, but hearing such praise from Chef Alain was both surprising and humbling. "Thank you, Chef," she managed to say, though her voice trembled slightly.

He nodded, acknowledging her gratitude. "I have a proposition for you", he continued, his eyes now gleaming with the excitement of what he was about to reveal. "There's a competition coming up—a prestigious event that draws attention from some of the finest chefs in Europe. The winner will receive a full scholarship to continue their studies here, as well as the opportunity to intern with one of the top patisseries in Paris. On behalf of our academy, we would like to nominate you."

Hema gasped, staring at him in utter disbelief. Of all the bright, talented chefs, she was the one being nominated. She couldn't believe her ears. This was an opportunity of a lifetime, something she hadn't even dared to dream of.

"I believe you have what it takes to compete," Chef Alain said before his tone turned serious. "But there's more. I've judged this competition before, and I even competed in it during the early days of my career. It's not just about skill; it's about innovation. You'll need to create something entirely new. It will be challenging, but I'm confident you're up for the task."

Hema felt a surge of adrenaline course through her. She was still unable to speak, and her mind was racing with thoughts and ideas. Chef Alain continued to outline the details of the competition, but she could barely focus, caught between disbelief and excitement. Finally, after a few minutes, Hema managed a breathless "Thank you.. so much, chef" before retreating to her workstation. She sat in stunned silence, her eyes flicking momentarily to the clock on the wall—it was 1:11 pm. She wondered if it were a gentle nudge from the universe, a sign of synchronicity, just when she needed it most. *Is this really happening?* She pinched herself, half-expecting to wake up from this dream.

The weeks leading up to the competition were some of the most intense and invigorating of Hema's life. After her conversation with Chef Alain, she knew she had to channel every ounce of her energy and creativity into crafting the perfect dish.

Each day, after classes, she would return to her small apartment, which had transformed into a makeshift laboratory. Here, she meticulously experimented with recipes, blending the rich, aromatic spices of Indian cuisine with the refined techniques she had learned at the academy. The space became a haven of creativity, filled with the scents of saffron, cumin, and butter as Hema experimented with ingredient combinations to craft a unique dish.

Her friends, Gerald and Christine, became her constant companions during these trials. Gerald always uplifted her spirits with the exuberance of someone discovering new flavours for the first time. Christine, with her sharp, discerning palate, offered the perfect counterbalance, helping Hema fine-tune the flavours with her feedback. Together, they formed an invaluable support system as the competition loomed closer.

One evening, they had gathered in Hema's apartment for another taste-testing session. The air was thick with the creamy scent of garlic-infused milk simmering on the stove. Hema presented her latest creation—a flaky croissant with a colourful, bold Indian filling. Gerald eagerly took a generous bite, only to have his eyes widen in shock as soon as the heat of the spices hit him full force.

"*Mamma mia,* Hema-latha! Are you trying to finish me off?" Gerald gasped, tears springing to his eyes as he fanned his mouth furiously.

Christine, lounging on the sofa with a glass of wine in hand, guffawed, nearly spilling her drink. "Oh, Gerald, you drama queen!" she teased, her voice laced with playful sarcasm. "What did you expect, biting into something Hema made without checking first? It's not exactly a plain old baguette, now is it?"

Hema chuckled in amusement, handing Gerald a glass of water. "I warned you it was hot," she said, shaking her head as Gerald gulped down the water.

"I thought I could handle it," Gerald spluttered, his face red as he tried to recover. "But this... this is like a volcano in my mouth!"

Christine grinned and raised her glass in a mock salute. "Well, if Hema's dish doesn't win the competition, at least we know it's effective as a weapon," she quipped, and the three of them burst out in laughter.

Still sniffling a bit from the spices, Gerald gave Hema a sheepish smile. "I may not survive this dish, but *davvero,* Hema, it's incredible. You're going to blow them away."

Christine nodded in agreement, "Yes, she will knock their socks off. To Hemalatha!"

As the laughter died down, a comfortable silence settled over the room. Hema felt a warm glow in her chest as she looked at her dish and then at her two friends, who had become like family. No matter the outcome of this competition, she knew she had already won.

The day of the competition arrived in a whirlwind of activity, each hour filled with anticipation. Hema could feel the tension in the air as she stood among the other contestants. The grand auditorium had been transformed into a culinary arena. Rows of workstations lined the stage, each arranged with gleaming utensils, fresh produce, and the focused energy of chefs ready to prove themselves. Her mind stormed with doubts and hopes, all at the same time as she reviewed her ingredients. *What if her dish wasn't good enough? What if she faltered at the crucial moment?* She shook her head, forcing herself to focus.

Hema worked at her station, her determination reflecting back at her from the polished stainless steel surfaces around her. The other contestants moved with a flurry of precise, well-practised motions, their culinary mastery on full display as they assembled their dishes. Thankfully, Hema's focus remained unwavering. The croissant had baked to perfection, crisp and golden, and now her hands moved with graceful assurance as she filled it with her signature spiced filling.
As the final moments ticked down, Hema carefully applied the finishing touches and then stepped back to admire her creation. She realized the dish, indeed,

stood out as a true testament to the unexpected fusion that had come to shape her new life.

When it was time for the judges to taste her dish, Hema's heart raced as they approached her station. Their expressions were unreadable. Each judge methodically took measured bites, considering the flavours. The seconds stretched on, and Hema's breath quickened as her heart hammered against her ribs.

There was a moment of weighted silence just as Hema's anxiety peaked, and then, almost in unison, the judges nodded in quiet approval. She exhaled deeply, the tension easing from her shoulders. She had poured her heart into this dish, and the judges' subtle acknowledgement felt like validation.

After what felt like an eternity, the judges returned to the stage to make the much-awaited announcement. The silence in the kitchen was deafening, punctuated only by the erratic throbbing of her pulse. And then, the final winner was announced—a young chef from Japan whose intricate sugar sculptures had captivated the judges with their artistry and technical prowess. Hema joined in the applause, feeling happy for the deserving winner, albeit a slight twinge of disappointment lingered in her heart. She had come so close.

But just as the ceremony was about to conclude, one of the judges stepped forward, holding a microphone in hand and clearing his throat. His voice cut through the loud applause. "Before we conclude..." he began, "we have a special recognition to announce", his tone commanding the attention of the entire hall. The audience fell into a hush, and Hema felt a flicker of anticipation.

"This year, we were particularly impressed by one chef's ability to merge her cultural heritage with the techniques she has mastered here. Her dish not only demonstrated exceptional skill but also told a story of creativity and passion," the judge continued, his gaze sweeping across the room before settling on Hema. "So, for the first time, we are pleased to present the Most Promising Chef Award to Hemalatha Rao."

A stunned silence followed, quickly replaced by enthusiastic applause as the spotlight turned to Hema. Her heart swelled with emotion as she stepped forward, her vision blurring slightly with unshed tears. As she accepted the award, the judge leaned in with a warm smile. "In addition," he announced, his voice resonating through the hall, "I would like to offer Hemalatha Rao an internship at my pastry atelier in Paris. Her talent and innovative approach are precisely what we look for in the next generation of great chefs."

The audience erupted in applause once more, and Hema's heart soared. She had not only gained recognition for her work but had also been given an opportunity that could change the course of her future. This had surpassed all her expectations. A sense of liberation welled inside her as she held her prize, basking in the glow of her achievement. The competition had been fierce, the journey challenging, but in that moment, standing on that stage, Hema knew it had all been worth it.

A few weeks later...

It was a Sunday evening, and the lively atmosphere in Christine's apartment stood in stark contrast to the gruelling intensity of the recent competition. The space buzzed with the hum of conversations and bursts of laughter as Hema, Gerald, Christine, and their fellow academy members gathered for a special celebration. Gerald, as always, was the life of the party, drawing everyone with his infectious energy. Meanwhile, Chef Alain stood quietly in a corner, a soft smile on his face as he observed from a distance.

Hema was in the kitchen, garnishing a platter of lamb croquettes she had prepared for the occasion. As she reached for a serving plate, her cell phone buzzed on the counter. Reaching over, she glanced at the screen, expecting it to be Ved or Meera, but her hand froze when she saw the name. It was Sanjeev. She hesitated for a moment before answering, her voice cautious. "Hello?"

"Hema", came the familiar voice on the other end, though it sounded different now—sober, almost pensive.

She waited, giving him the chance to continue.

"I... I saw the news about the competition. Congratulations," Sanjeev said, his words tentative.

"Thank you", Hema replied after a few seconds, determined to remain composed.

There was a pause, and when Sanjeev spoke again, his tone had softened. "I heard about the dish you made.." Another pause, longer this time. "I just... I wanted to say that I'm proud of you, Hema. You've accomplished something amazing."
Hema stood silently for a moment, a tangled knot of emotions rising inside her. Yet, her voice was calm and firm. "Thank you, Sanjeev. I've worked hard to get here."

Silence.

"I need to go," she said with a touch of finality after a few seconds. "My friends have thrown me a party for—" Her voice faltered slightly.
"I know", he interjected, his voice an echo of sadness.

A long silence followed again, neither of them able to speak.

"Yes, you should get back," Sanjeev finally said, his tone filled with remorse. I just... I just wanted to say I'm sorry for everything, Hema. I wish things had been different, but—" He trailed off, waiting for a response that didn't come. "I... I wish you the best."
Hema took a deep breath, feeling the weight of his words settle over her. After a long moment, she said with a gentle tone, "We all make our choices, Sanjeev. I've made mine."

There was another pause, and then Sanjeev replied, his voice resigned. "I'm glad, Hema. I really am."

The call ended. As Hema put her phone down, her eyes drifted to the clock on the kitchen wall—it was 11:11 pm, a time she had come to appreciate as a sign of new beginnings. There were still a few minutes left until her 46th birthday, she thought, whispering a silent prayer.

Hema was about to grab the plate of croquettes when a strong hand reached out, taking it from her instead. Startled, she looked up to see Chef Alain standing beside her, his green eyes narrowing slightly as he watched her with concern.
"Sorry, I didn't mean to startle you," he said, his voice deep and steady. "Is everything okay?"
Hema offered with a soft smile. "Yes, it is", she said. "Everything's fine". She believed it.

Chef Alain studied her for a second, then looked toward the counter. "How about a drink?" he asked, a hint of anticipation in his voice.
She smiled a little wider now. "I'd like that."
"Okay."
His movements were swift and effortless as he deftly mixed the ingredients to create a cocktail of understated elegance. As he handed her the glass, their fingers brushed lightly, and he raised his glass in a toast.
"To new beginnings?" he proposed with a grin.

"To new beginnings", Hema echoed, clinking her glass against his in a nod to the future.

They took a sip, savouring the moment before turning and walking back into the living room, where their friends awaited. Hema's heart was whole. She glanced out at the city lights twinkling beyond the window, knowing she had created a place that was truly her own, and one that no one could take away from her.

www.ingramcontent.com/pod-product-compliance
Lightning Source LLC
La Vergne TN
LVHW041103150826
845673LV00007B/1896

* 9 7 9 8 8 9 5 4 4 8 9 6 0 *